January Embers

A Year in Paradise

Hildred Billings

BARACHOU PRESS

January Embers

Published: 11th January 2019
Publisher: Barachou Press

Chapter 1

MIKAIYA

A woman couldn't drive for five miles in Oregon without the winter rains splashing against her windshield.

"Watch out!" Skylar grabbed the *oh shit* handle as they may or may not have *slightly* hydroplaned into the other highway lane. Luckily, there were no other cars on the road. Driver Mikaiya had forgotten how desolate some of these roads became on early winter nights. Throw on some headlights reflecting the rain... and, well, was it a wonder she didn't see the giant wave of water flooding from a nearby creek?

"We're fine!" Mik had a death grip on her steering wheel. *Thank God for a sturdy truck!* The tarp covering her furniture and plastic totes fluttered in the wind and rain, but they should be protected as long as Mik didn't flip over the truck. *Where are the other cars?* A little rain wouldn't stop the locals of Paradise Valley from getting where they needed to go. Was there nuclear fallout nearby? Did a tree block the highway up ahead? Mikaiya had not missed the high winds that powered through the area during the winter. They were close enough to the coast to get the worst of it, and high up enough in the Coast Range to get dumped on before anyone else in the county. *Did. Not. Miss. This.* Yet Mikaiya had learned to drive in the worst of Oregon's winter weather. Her friends in Portland were total babies when a little rain fell. If only they could see her now!

Skylar covered her face with her hands as they took a sharp turn down the hill. The cedar trees shielded the worst of the rain on this part of the road, but that also meant critters taking shelter were likely to run out into the road at any moment. Already, Mik had seen an unfortunate amount of roadkill on the side of the highway. Something else her city friends were not as familiar with.

"Are we almost there?" Skylar squeaked.

"About five more miles." Mikaiya would have called her grandmother to tell her they were almost there, but nobody, including the forest rangers with their satellite phones, could get reception. "Sorry we left so late. I should have listened to the weather reports." One would never guess they left Portland as early as two that afternoon. The sky was cloudy yet bright, but as soon as they left the Willamette Valley, the rain and gloom arrived. Paradise Valley was only a couple hours from Portland, but between the rain, the traffic farther out, and the multiple pee breaks Skylar insisted on as things got hairier... it was pitch black by the time they got this far four days after New Year's.

Mik had little choice about when she moved back to her hometown, however. Her contract at the marketing agency in Portland lasted until Christmas, which she spent with the close friends she had made over the years while working for a firm that had international sportswear, food processing, and medical equipment manufacturers for clients. The stress had been so bad that Mikaiya forgot what it was like to have a personal life outside of her best buddies in the building where she worked. Dating? Impossible. After a nervous breakdown that left her bereft for a few weeks, she decided to not renew her contract and figure out something else to do with her life. She had money in the bank and... well, she had her grandmother, Abby, the woman who helped raise her in Paradise Valley.

When Abby suffered a major stroke in September, Mik thought it was the end. Yet her resilient grandmother pulled through. The fact she personally asked Mik to move back home and help her around the house meant things were bad. Yet wasn't it a sign from the universe that she had quit her job around the time her grandmother needed her?

In Paradise Valley... the place Mikaiya had left, hoping to never return...

She sighed. The rain let up a bit. A road sign assured her that "Paradise is Only Three Miles Away." Not to be confused with the *other* Paradise, Oregon, of course.

"We're almost there," she reassured Skylar, one of her best friends who agreed to move to the small town with her. Like Mik, Skylar needed a serious change of pace from the chilly, strange vibe of Portland. When Mikaiya reminded her heterosexual friend that Paradise Valley was originally a lesbian commune that now boasted one of the highest populations of queer women in the state, Skylar merely commented that it really did sound like paradise. Because someone had no interest in dealing with men and dating for a good, long while. "I hope my grandma's got a fire going. Hey, at least it ain't snowin'!"

Skylar groaned. "We're not even there yet, and you already sound like a hick."

"Don't worry, hon. You'll pick it up quick enough."

"God smite me if I ever have a faux-Texan twang!"

Mikaiya chuckled. She finally let up on the windshield wipers and let out a sigh of relief that they were almost to the city limits.

They rounded one of the last major curves leading into town… and Mik was compelled to hit the brakes.

"Jesus!" Skylar grabbed her seatbelt and braced herself against the glove compartment. "What happened?"

Even through the rain, the tell-tale signs of a car accident were ever-present. Flashing warning lights. Bright orange cones. A giant ambulance and a cop car with their lights on. They had probably just missed the fire truck.

"Wow. Hope nobody was seriously hurt." Mik was stuck behind the wreckage. No wonder she hadn't seen any cars coming the other way. Both vehicles involved in this crash took up the whole two-lane highway. A sedan was flipped, and an old, rusty truck was halfway into a ditch, the driver revving the engine and spinning the back wheels, trying to get the hell out. Mik was grateful that she didn't immediately recognize anyone. Would've been grand if the first thing she saw when returning to her childhood home was her second grade teacher wrenched from her car with the jaws of life.

The driver of the other car sat in the back of the ambulance, a cold compress on her head and an EMT giving her a look over. One of the other EMTs caught sight of Mikaiya and Skylar and sauntered over. Maybe tourists would have assumed that was a self-assured young man, but Mik immediately recognized the cool gait of one of Paradise Valley's many native butches. *Great. So when I'm not fearing for my life on this highway, I'm getting all hot and bothered by the locals.* Here was hoping this nice woman had a wedding band on her left hand. Mik had gone so long without dating that she was liable to jump the first willing woman she came across in Paradise Valley.

Now there's a good way to reunite with my second grade teacher…

"Sorry about the mess here." The EMT leaned inside the cab of Mik's truck after she rolled down the window. Rain continued to pound the pavement and the top of the EMT's head, but nobody, least of all a couple of native Oregonians, were perturbed by a little wet on the forehead. "Tow truck will be here soon, so we'll hopefully have at least one lane open for traffic."

"Thanks. I hope nobody was hurt."

"Looks worse than it apparently is." The EMT sniffed. "If you're in a hurry, there's an old dirt road about a half mile back that turns into Ar..."

"Arizona Street?" Mik interrupted. "Oh, yeah, I remember that one."

"You do, huh?" That earned her a pearly-white smile. *I used to know a sweet girl who smiled like that.* A pang hit Mikaiya right in the heart. Damn. She knew she was going to think about *her* as soon as she was back in that familiar wasteland, but wasn't expecting to be reminded of her first big love before she saw a building.

Mik cleared her throat. "I'm from here."

"Oh? Don't recognize... you..." The EMT took a step back with a scoff. So much for not recognizing her. "Mikaiya Marcott."

Mikaiya's eyes widened. *Oh, my God, who is this? An old classmate of mine?* Or was the EMT older than she looked in the rainy dark? Did she know Mikaiya as a little kid? Why couldn't Mik recognize a person who clearly knew her? Had ten years really been enough time for her to forget what it was like living in a tiny Oregonian town?

"Uh, yup, that's me. Heh?"

The EMT put her hands on her hips. Damn, wasn't she beyond formidable in that heavy rain jacket, those hefty boots, and the hat on her long head? *She looks like she's about to kick my ass!* The worst part? Mik had a huge soft spot for strong butches who could throw her over their shoulder and cart her off somewhere. (Preferably, to bed.) This was going south, fast. First, the terrible omens of the rain and the crash that almost ended someone's life. Now? Mik was pissing off the locals, and she didn't remember who they were! *I was a kid when I left! How am I supposed to know what kids back then look like now?*

"Welcome home, Mikkie."

Did the rain stop? Or did Mik's heart stop beating, and now she could no longer hear, see, or smell a damn thing?

Oh. My. God.

This wasn't some stranger she barely knew as a kid. This was fate. This was hell.

This was Ariana Mura, the girl Mikaiya dated back in high school. The girl she left behind the day they graduated. The girl whose heart she probably broke.

Didn't look like anyone was going to break anything of Ari's anytime soon, now.

Chapter 2

ARIANA

Well, look at what the dog dragged in from the garbage pile.

Ariana was already in an uncomfortable situation. Racing to a scene in the middle of a rainstorm was nothing new for the EMT, but did she like it? No! Who the hell wanted to stand for forty-five minutes in the pouring rain while exhaust fumes filled the air and angry drivers honked at her to get a “move on?” That was when she had the luxury of taking in that deplorable scenery. Oftentimes, someone was hurt enough that all of her focus was on getting them stabilized and to the county hospital before it was too late. Tonight's accident looked bad, but only the driver of the sedan suffered any kind of minor injury. The boys had her possible concussion under control. They would take her to the hospital when she was ready to move, but there wasn't much else for Ariana to do than assist Deputy Greenhill with directing traffic.

Now, *this?* Ari envied the woman sitting in the back of the ambulance. What Ari would give to have a concussion right about now!

Mikaiya. Marcott. Here. In the flesh. In some fancy truck with a bed full of items and another girl in the passenger seat. Who was she? Mikaiya's latest victim? Some hapless city-slickin' soul that had no idea what she was in for? Then again, some of the townsfolk definitely thought that the Portlanders had no souls and deserved whatever they got. Because both Mikkie and the girl beside her *screamed* Portland, from their thin, department-store bought plaid shirts and fancy haircuts. With one glance, Ari could tell that Mik's hands were softer than a baby's butt. One didn't have to do hard labor to get calloused hands while living in a small town. Even the people who typed on laptops all day still had to cut firewood and change their oil. Mik looked like she hadn't done a hard day's of labor since she used to work on her uncle's farm.

Great. Ari really was a masochist, huh? Because now she was thinking about losing her virginity to Mik in the loft of her uncle's barn. *Got hay up my ass, but I was young and dumb enough to think it was worth it!* Ariana hated how flustered she already was after two seconds of recognizing the girl who had stomped all over her heart and taken a giant dump on her soul.

"The fuck you doing back here?"

Mikaiya gasped. Ari instantly regretted saying it. Like that, anyway. *Well, now she knows I'm still a resentful bitch, so I've got that going for me.* At least Ari wasn't cowering before her. The old Ari would have. The one who spent the whole summer after senior year crying in her bed. *Then I chopped off my hair. Started hitting the gym. Finally enrolled into a program that would give me a life of saving other people's lives instead of tearing down my own*. That was the power of a broken heart.

She had thought Mikaiya a ghost. Now, here she was, with PORTLAND stamped all over her, thinking she could ever belong in Paradise Valley again. Damn. She was here because of her grandmother, wasn't she? Abby Marcott didn't deserve a granddaughter like Mikkie.

"I'm moving back for a while." Mik played it cool, although Ari wanted to believe that her ex trembled like a frightened child deep, deep down. She should. She should fear the fuck out of Ariana Mura now that she knew how to get her point across and wasn't afraid to smack the shit out of this bitch if she tried her crap again. *I make it sound like she abused me...* No, it had never been like that. Mik was a weak-hearted git, and Ari was too stupid and too in love to realize that following her girlfriend was a good idea. Mik's dreams of leaving rural Oregon finally came true. Part of Ari's deciding to stay and become a core member of the community was to spite the traitor.

"Your grandma?" Ari forced a more neutral tone. The rain washed off her face. She could no longer feel it now that an old, haunted visage stared back at her from the cab of a brand-new truck. "I know about what happened."

"Yes, well..." Good! That was a squeak in her voice! She definitely deserved that! "Anyway, I guess I better be turning around and finding that road. I've got four-wheel drive, so I should be okay."

Like I care. Ari cared enough that she didn't want to be called to save her ex's life, but she could be a vindictive ass-butt when the moment called for it.

"Now's your chance to turn around before any other cars come." *And get the fuck out of my town.* Ari would treat this as a shitty dream. Her ex, a rainy night, and an accident that could've been a lot worse. Bad enough Ari would be doing paperwork past dinnertime. Now here was Ms. Too Good For You sashaying back into Paradise Valley like she was Sappho's gift to lesbian kind. "I won't tell Deputy Greenhill that you're making an illegal U-turn."

Mikaiya narrowed her eyes. Oh, she knew what her ex meant. The message was as loud and clear now as it had been a decade ago. "Greenhill, huh? So Cadence really became a cop?"

"Yup. Now she's deputy in Paradise Valley. So don't piss off our nice lunch lady."

Mik turned to her friend in the passenger seat. Ari wasn't going to ask who the stranger was. She didn't want to know, or care. *I don't want the details on your new girlfriend, Mik.* Ari would rather eat the mud her ex was about to tear up down that dirt road on her way to Arizona Street. Probably would get to her old house faster than the highway, anyway.

"Thanks." Mik shifted gears and, turning around outside the window to get a better view of the highway behind her, backed the truck up to make that illegal U. "See you around, Ari."

God, I hope not! Ari gave them a half-hearted wave before turning back to meet Deputy Greenhill in the road. Eventually, the taillights from Mik's truck disappeared around the curve.

"Someone you know?" Cadence Greenhill, the only woman in town possibly tougher than Ari, asked. "Takes a lot to make you turn a shoulder to a stranger."

Ari gritted her teeth. "You'll never guess who's back in town."

"Hm?" Greenhill glanced down the dark highway. "Hope it's not that Ben McLaughlin. Thought we ran his ass out of here once and for all."

A laugh shot out of Ari's mouth. *Oh, little miss Soft Butch will love to know she was mistaken for Ben Freaking McLaughlin!* Ben had written himself into the annals of infamy when he opened a shop in Paradise Valley in the hopes of finding the bisexual woman of his dreams. Better if she was a lesbian he could turn to his dick-side. Took five years and half a town of pissed off lesbians who were sick of his fetishizing shit before he finally took the hint and shuttered up his shop and got the hell out of town.

"I wish!" Ari scoffed. "That was Mikaiya Marcott. Remember her?"

The deputy took a step back. "You're kidding. Little Mikkie? The softball shortstop?"

Ari grunted.

"Your ex-girlfriend who..."

"Yeah, her!" Ari marched to the ambulance, where she shoved aside fellow EMT Brendon and took over. "Y'all better give me something to do. Now."

Ariana always did best when she had something productive to take her mind off the shit. Riding in the back with this poor woman on their way to the county hospital would be a great way to take her mind off that fuckhead who stole her heart – then her faith in love.

Chapter 3

MIKAIYA

"You seriously cannot believe how many lesbians there are here." Skylar followed that with laughter as she moseyed into the living room. Behind her, Mikaiya rooted through the pantry, taking stock of what her grandmother already had and what needed to be purchased at the market later that day. "It's a veritable Lilith Fair, 24/7. I seriously heard Melissa Etheridge playing in the town square. *Yes,* they have a town square! You've gotta come see it!"

Mikaiya rolled her eyes. She didn't know who Skylar talked to on the phone, nor did she care. Hearing that was enough to make her retreat back into the pantry with her cell phone. The notetaking app was filled with food they desperately needed now that there was a break in the weather. Ever since coming into town and seeing that car wreck first thing, she had been wary of driving while the rains continued to pour and the wind whipped up the trees into a frenzy. In Portland, she could hop a bus or walk a few blocks in the rain. Here in Paradise Valley, she had to drive if she wanted to avoid getting drenched – or twisting her ankle on the uneven sidewalks.

All right… so I have an ulterior motive for not wanting to go into town. She didn't know if she might see Ariana. The thought of bumping into her, anywhere, made her want to hurl.

"Grandma?" Mikaiya called down the hallway of her grandmother's ranch house. "Do you still drink Diet Coke?"

"Does a bear shit in the woods?" came a cracking voice from the master bedroom.

"Does a bear shit in the woods…" Skylar repeated. "Ha! Love it. Oh, not you, Jeremy.

Was talking about Mik's grandmother. She's *real* country."

Mikaiya needed to get out of here. Preferably without Skylar on her ass, who was supposed to be looking for a job but instead spent most of her days on her phone. *I give her another three months before she's rushing back to Portland.* Sure, Sky was having fun *now* in a town with nothing but lesbians, but she'd get bored, eventually. Either that, or she'd piss off the wrong people by being Straighty McStraighterton strolling through the town square gawking at the female couples making out beneath the bright blue mountain skies.

Abby awaited her granddaughter in the bedroom. The old analog TV played *Family Matters* reruns while Abby futilely attempted to knit a hat. Her wrinkled hands were determined to stay anything but idle while she caught up on her post-stroke bed rest. This was a woman who had grown up on a farm and was used to spending every day of her life being active, both in mind and body. When she wasn't beating everyone in the daily crossword puzzle race, she was leading hikes down Wolf's Hill and tending to her vegetable garden. Abby hadn't moved into town so she could enjoy "town life." She merely wanted to raise her kids in a place that actually had a school, although Paradise Valley shared a high school with neighboring Roundabout. *The high school I went to with Ari...*

Someone saw the look on Mikaiya's face when she stepped in to talk groceries.

"About time you're finally going to the store," Abby muttered. The pink yarn in her hands refused to bow to her whim. "I thought it would be another dinner of rice and gravy. You didn't bother with vegetables last night!"

"I couldn't find your stores until this morning."

"I could've told you where they were."

"I didn't want to wake you from your nap."

Abby held up her hands in defeat. "Let me take a look at that list. You probably forgot the grass-fed steaks from the butcher's."

Mikaiya sat on the edge of her grandmother's bed while Abby muttered over the list she deemed unworthy. While Mik loved her grandmother, she could be a real hardass. Just like her son and daughter. *Mom and Uncle Jake.* There had been no permanent father figure in Mik's life. Not aside from Uncle Jake, who recruited her working girl hands every school break. *He hated Paradise Valley.* Enough that he eventually killed himself with a heart attack. Mik's mother had also died long ago. For most of her adolescence, Grandma Abby and Uncle Jake were her only family. Until Ari came along in high school...

Jake had done good messing with that, too.

"By the way," Mikaiya grumbled, "I ran into Ari the first night here. I thought you told me she was *gone.*" One of the only ways Mik was coming back to Paradise Valley was if she thought the odds of bumping into her ex were slim to none. There were other people she wasn't keen on seeing, either, but Ari was Numero Uno on the list.

Abby snorted before handing the list back to her granddaughter. "She *is* gone. The Ariana you used to know, anyway."

"No kidding."

"That little scrawny girl hasn't been around for several years. Ain't nobody but her mother remembering her that way."

"You know what I meant when I asked."

"So? You wanted to know if the Ariana Mura you used to date was still around. She ain't. That Ariana is somebody brand-new to you. Not to anyone else in town, but hey, you haven't been here since Christmas of 2012."

A three day affair. Mikaiya never left the house out of fear of seeing somebody else she knew. "She was really pissed to see me."

"She was probably working and you interrupted her! Like you interrupted my knitting time!" Abby shooed her granddaughter out of her room. "Go on, get! I want some Ho-Hos for my afternoon snack, and I *know* we're out of those. Take that weird friend of yours, too. She's so loud on her phone that I have half a mind to knit her one and purl her two."

However, Mikaiya had no desire to take Skylar with her to the grocery store. Mik needed time to think for herself. To sort out her feelings about being back in town. Skylar only made her stick out more, because Sky *was* an out-of-towner who drew attention to herself. Mikaiya needed to start blending in again. Wasn't like the town had changed that much since she was last there. A few buildings had fresh coats of paint, the old hardware store was now a café, and there was a giant pothole at the end of the Marcotts' street, but beyond that? Paradise Valley, like most American small towns, didn't change for a shift in the earth.

That was for the best when it came to blending in and acting like she knew what she was about. That was for the worst when it came to the *people.* In her four days since being home, more than one older person had come by the house to exclaim that they remembered when Mik was "just this tall." Too bad she never recognized these people who seemed to know her when she was still picking her nose. As for the kids that were now adults? Shit, they recognized her too, but she sure as hell didn't remember them! Maybe moving to a city like Portland had colored her ability to remember people. When a woman was constantly bombarded by strangers' faces every time she walked down the street, she stopped acknowledging anyone. Including her own friends.

She hopped in her truck and avoided the giant pothole on her way to the market. Luckily, that was the easiest place in town to stick her head down and avoid eye contact. People looking for a conversation quickly found them in other shoppers. That included people who might recognize her. Like the clerk working the only lane open at that time of day.

"Mikaiya? Mikaiya Marcott?"

Mik looked up from her wallet as the clerk scanned the groceries and threw them into the canvas bags someone always carried in her truck. "Uh... yeah, that's me."

"Dang, how long has it been!" Bushy brown hair and a smile as wide as Kansas pinged something in Mik's faraway memory, but she couldn't remember who this girl was for the life of her. "I haven't seen you since ya graduated from high school like... ten years ago!"

"Yeah, it's been a while." Mik cleared her throat after sticking her debit card into the chip reader. *Well, that's another change in this town. Chip readers.* Didn't stop the person in front of her from writing the longest check in history. "Sorry, I don't remember..." She caught herself the moment she saw the nametag on the girl's green blouse. "Anem?"

"Hell, yeah! So you do remember me?" Anem giggled when she saw the nametag on her blouse. "Oh. Right."

"No, I remember you. We played softball together at Clark High. Outfield, right?"

"Not as popular as the best shortstop Clark had seen in a dozen years, but yeah! Gee, you haven't changed a bit, huh? Bet you couldn't recognize me because I got my teeth fixed."

Right. Anem Singer used to get relentlessly teased for her big teeth and bushy hair. The hair was a little more tamed in her adulthood, but the teeth? Huh. Yeah. Straight as arrows. Mikaiya definitely recognized her now. She also recalled that while Anem was one rambunctious little squirt on the high school softball team, she was also nice. Here's hoping that remained true.

"You visiting, or…"

"I've moved back in with my grandma a to help her recover," Mikaiya said.

"Riiiiight, I heard about that! Tell her get well for me, will ya? She once gave me some fresh veggies from her garden, and I still think about them all the time."

"Yeah. Sure." Mikaiya grabbed her bags and high-tailed it out of there before other shoppers realized who she was. Her truck was parked in the back of the lot, however, because she always hated getting so close to the door that pedestrians blocked her way when she tried backing out. It had been a bigger problem in cramped Portland parking lots. Here in Paradise Valley, however, she was more likely to bump into someone way out in the boonies.

Someone like Ariana Mura.

There she was, jumping out of her old pickup, dressed in the same jeans and boots from the other night, but now wrapped in a thick black sweatshirt that covered her muscles and showed off the undercut gracing the top of her head. *Jesus. I still can't believe that's her..* The Ariana Mik dated ten years ago was a slender girl who wore threadbare dresses and kept her dark hair in loose ponytails. She experimented with makeup because, as she liked to say, "*I want to know the perfect shade of lipstick for kissin' you with.*" Grownup, EMT Ari looked more like a big, burly sister instead of the sweet little femme Mikaiya used to bring to her uncle's farm for some privacy.

Ari must have sensed Mikaiya's presence, for she stopped halfway across the parking lot.

A chill thundered down Mik's spine, zapping her in the ass and kicking her right in the crotch. *Jesus. Mary. Joseph.* That was the holy trinity she called upon when she met those ferocious blue eyes from only a few feet away. *She's prettier than I remember.* Maybe that wasn't the right word to think as she watched Ari slowly make her way across the parking lot and into the store, but Mikaiya couldn't help it. Ariana Mura was still as gorgeous as the last day Mikaiya saw her smiling.

Man, fuck this town. Mikaiya hopped into her truck and refused to leave her grandmother's house for the rest of the day.

Chapter 4

ARIANA

Ari popped open a beer and settled into her side of the couch. “C’mon, man, skip all that commentator fluff,” she scoffed before bringing her can to her lips. “I wanna watch the game before I crash.”

Roommate (and coworker) Brendon hit the fast forward button on the remote. The talking football heads animatedly yucked it up while the couch sank beneath the weight of another person. Both Ariana and Brendon propped their feet up on the coffee table and leaned back with their beers. Cold pizza chilled on paper plates. Ari was so damn tired that she didn’t have the energy to grab a slice of last night’s leftovers.

Was it really last night when we grabbed pizza from the parlor? Because it feels like earlier today. Make it stop. Why was Ari so tired, anyway? Not like work was any worse than usual. She responded to her fair share of car wrecks along the hallway – and one fender bender in town that gave a guy whiplash – but most of her shifts had been sitting around waiting for something to come in. When Ariana wasn't figuring out her schedule for the required training, she was scrolling through Instagram or forcing herself to read that month's Stephen King Book Club selection. *I can't only read* It *so many damn times. Clown. Kids. Some weirdly uncomfortable scenes that will be all anyone talks about at the meeting this week.* She wasn't reading it as much as she was giving herself a refresher. *It* was one of the first King books she read back when she was in her depressive funk, and the one that made her read more until she was convinced to join the book club at the library.

Mikaiya. That's why I'm so freakin' tired all the time.

How could Ari get any sleep when her ex was back in town? Someone might as well put a bullet in her chest and stomp a steel-toed boot into the back of her neck. That's what it felt like every time she crossed paths with Mik, and it happened more than once in the past week.

The grocery parking lot. The post office. At the four-way stop on the edge of town. *I got there first, but she went on ahead!* That had been the last straw. After that, Ariana sequestered herself in the house she shared with two roommates when she didn't have to be at work. If she and Mik were going to share the same town, she would need a little time to practice her reactions.

Too bad she didn't have a hot girlfriend at the moment. One badass enough to make Mik quake in her fancy Doc Martens and realize what a fuckup she was, anyway.

"You okay over there, Sleeping Beauty?"

Ariana grabbed her slice of pizza and sighed. She had been staring at Monday Night Football for the past hour, yet not a single play or commercial had registered in her brain. There was only dissociating from one of the worst nights of her life.

Who knew she had been *that* traumatized? Ari hadn't acted like this about her first major breakup since it happened. Was Mikaiya some kind of unwitting trigger? Then again, Ari wasn't convinced her ex had a soul, so...

"Sorry," she said to Brendon. "Thinking about stuff."

"Like your ex-ladyfriend being back in town?"

"How the hell did you hear about that?" Ari snapped.

"It's a small town. Word gets around. Everyone knows."

Of course they did. Who narked? Was it Greenhill to her wife? Sally Greenhill was the biggest blabbermouth that side of the Willamette River. Then again, it could've been anyone. Mik had been out and about, obviously. She had probably bumped into and talked to lots of the townspeople she once knew so well. Who didn't know about their history? Even newcomers who settled in long enough eventually heard about what "the cute EMT" went through in high school.

"What really happened, huh?" Brendon asked. He was one of those more recent newcomers. Only three years in Paradise Valley, and he still didn't know the Ballad of Mikaiya Marcott and Ariana Mura. Then again, this was a guy who often forgot that Ariana once had a ponytail and a closet full of dresses.

"You're not watching the game, huh?"

"We're up twenty points. You think I'm that entranced right now?" Brendon chuckled. "I'd rather hear about your high school drama."

"It's not that funny, honestly."

"Geez, sorry."

Sighing, Ari put aside her meager dinner and attempted to watch the game. It immediately went to commercial, and it was all she could do to keep from screaming.

"Fine," she said, "but if I tell you, you gotta promise to not tell anyone. Ever."

"But everyone already knows, right?"

"There are lots of different versions to the 'story' out there, Bren."

"Uh huh. So, which one's your favorite?"

Favorite? *Favorite?* Like she could stand to talk about it, let alone entertain the versions where Mikaiya dumped her because of a boy? *It's bad enough everyone talks. They have to insult me while they do it?* Of course they did.

"Mik and I went to school together." Clark High School represented both Paradise Valley and neighboring Roundabout. Back then, Ariana lived in Roundabout, so she never had the chance to meet Mikaiya until then. Probably for the best. Considering how hard their chemistry hit once Mik got out of a relationship with another girl and Ariana approached her at school, meeting any younger may have proved detrimental to Ari's health. "We dated for two years, from the summer before junior year until graduation. She was my first."

Brendon didn't ask questions, but his raising eyebrows made Ari shake her head. *Can't believe I told him that.*

"Dunno what to tell you. It was typical teen stuff, man." Going to the only movie theater in town, driving to the beach as soon as Mik got her license, hanging out to do homework and watching every softball game in the county… for a pair of girls who grew up in a school district populated by lesbian moms, it was about as good as it got. The only hang-up was Mikaiya's uncle, Jake. He was an atypical homophobe in a place that did not cater to them. Whenever Mikaiya spent her summers helping out on the family farm, she was explicitly told to *not* bring girls over. Yet she did, anyway. Did he think he could keep Mik from seeing her girlfriend for a *whole* summer, when they were so close, anyway? Yeah, right. Ariana was always sneaking out to the farm to fool around when Uncle Jake wasn't around. Sometimes she helped out, too. Mik always brushed off the heat hanging above them as if it were nothing. As if Uncle Jake hadn't already spent a few nights in the county lockup because he assaulted women he didn't "agree with." Ariana didn't have a grand imagination, so when her mind wandered to what Jake might do if he ever caught her on the farm… she didn't think it was too farfetched.

I could take him now.

"Kids in love do dumb stuff, right?" Ari continued. "Well, we were the dumbest. After I had a freak out that she was going off to college, we decided to get married graduation night. We were going to drive to Vegas. You can see how stupid we sounded, because I don't think you can drive from here to Vegas in one night."

"No, you sure can't, Ari."

"Well, graduation day came. We had the pomp and circumstance, but when it came time to meetup to head out of town, she never showed up." Ari shrugged. "That was it."

Brendon let out a low whistle. "She wasn't held up somewhere or had an accident?"

"Nope. After I stayed up all night panicking, I found out that she left without me."

"To Vegas?"

"No idea. She skipped out on town, and we never saw each other until this past week."

Brendon sat back in the couch, half-drunk can of beer resting atop his knee and face completely blown off his head in shock. "Whoa."

"Yup. She stood me up. Didn't have the balls to tell me why, or that she didn't really want to go through with it. Simply didn't show up, while I sat there feeling like the biggest jackass in the world."

"That's rough, Ari." Brendon tapped his chin. "Was this before or *after* your great transformation I've heard about?"

How much could one woman roll her eyes without damaging her brain? Because Ari was on the verge of pushing her eyeballs out of their sockets. "Before."

"Uh huh..."

"Why people insist on talking about that, I have no idea."

"I've seen the pics, Ari. You were like some scrawny little sunflower child who couldn't lift her own pup over her head, let alone *me*."

"First of all, that only happened once and probably won't happen again without me seriously hurting myself." It had been pure boneheadedness that made her prove her womanly strength to the recent EMT recruit. Yet the sheer amount of pride Ari experienced when she heaved this guy over her head could be felt across the county. "Second, it's not that weird. People completely change when they grow up all the time."

"Sure, but it explains a lot about why you underwent such a *drastic* transformation." Brendon shrugged. "Girl breaks your heart, makes you feel vulnerable, you bulk up so nobody hurts you again."

A thousand words echoed across Ari's mind, but the ones that came out of her mouth were nothing better than, "Shut up!" She chucked her empty beer can at his head.

What she hated the most was how right he was. That fact continued to linger in her head as they finished watching a lackluster game and hit the showers before bed. Ari convinced herself that she wasn't bothered by her roommate's words or the truth behind them. Even as she stared at the back of her shampoo bottle for fifteen minutes, forgetting that she was supposed to put some of that on her head. She also forgot to close the blinds on the bathroom window. She should be so lucky that her neighbors weren't taking the trash out when she hopped from the shower in her naked glory.

I really did this to protect myself, didn't I? She thought that while brushing her teeth and rubbing moisturizer into her body. The woman staring back at her hardly looked like the girl who went to Clark High School and dated a heartbreaker named Mikaiya Marcott. It was more than hitting the gym and cutting off her hair. It was the way she carried herself, as if she were the most powerful woman on the block, and anyone who crossed her would get a giant boot up their ass. Her clothes were either gender neutral or coded masculine to the point so many people outside of Paradise Valley mistook her for a man. Her voice was deeper and her outlook far more cynical than teenaged Ariana. *I refused to let myself be pushed around like that again.* While it was true that most kids grew up into totally different adults, the reason everyone commented on Ariana's transformation was because the people who watched her grow up hardly recognized her as the same girl.

No wonder Mikaiya hadn't known Ari on that dark, rainy night a week ago.

"No fuckhead is gonna break your heart again, huh?" Ari said that to her reflection in the mirror. A streak of her hand allowed her to see the square face and serious eyebrows that now made women swoon like girls used to swoon over Mik. Back in high school, her soft butch approach to jeans, boots, and plaid had been the ticket to getting girls like Ariana, who appreciated the feminine touches to a traditionally butch look. Now it was old hat. Half the women in Paradise Valley were some flavor of butch. Hell, Deputy Greenhill gave Ari a run for *her* money. There was a reason that little town attracted so many likeminded women. It wasn't merely a chance to have a dating life with a taste of country living. It was the assurance that nobody would fuck you up because you really had tits beneath that vest.

Yet Ari had grown up in the area and *still* got fucked up.

I wonder what she thinks of me now. Mikaiya had a sleeker haircut and shinier boots, but she would never be mistaken for someone other than the star shortstop on the Clark High softball team. There was a difference between aging and what Ariana went through. *She sure doesn't want anything to do with me.* Wasn't that a good thing?

Why would Ari *want* Mik bothering her after a decade of deafening silence?

She tossed on a baggy shirt and headed to her room, where she collapsed into her bed and set her alarm for the next day's shift. Yet she couldn't drift off to sleep. She was too busy staring into the darkness, wondering where the hell she was and how quickly she could get away from that tightness in her throat again.

She couldn't stop thinking about Mikaiya. What they used to have as kids. How stupid they had been to think about running off to get married. How stupid Ari had been to believe her. *Why wouldn't I have believed her? She never lied to me before. She never treated me with anything but kindness and respect.*

That was the part that always hurt the most. There had been no warning signs. Not even with Ari's current hindsight could she see any clues leading up to that terrible night. It was as if Mikaiya had been plucked out of the night. If it weren't for Abby telling a distraught little Ari that Mik had gone to Portland, she would have filed the missing person's report for herself.

Instead, *she* was the one who went missing. For months. For a year. Ari was almost twenty years old when she signed up for a few online courses to start working toward her EMT career. By then, she was already transforming herself into the kind of woman whose heart could not be broken.

So why was her pillow wet with tears?

Chapter 5

MIKAIYA

"You're going to get yourself killed," Abby said, head poking out of her bay window. "And I'm going to laugh."

Across from her, Skylar snickered in front of her laptop. The two of them had become best buds since the day Abby was no longer bedridden and could move around her house at will. She often took to sitting at the table in the bay window, knitting needles hard at work while Joni Mitchell played on the stereo and tea brewed on the stove. Skylar started calling her "my adopted grandma," and relied on Abby's advice and ability to serve as an excellent reference in the great job hunt. Skylar had a few leads, but nothing had come from them yet.

Paradise Valley was worse than the average small town when it came to networking to get the most mundane of jobs. It was *really* a "who you know" kind of town. Abby was invaluable, but she hadn't scored Sky a job yet.

Probably a good thing Mikaiya wasn't in the business of finding herself a job yet. Instead, she spent her days fixing up the house, including taking a hard look at the gutters the day before. As soon as the most recent rains cleared, she brought a ladder out of the garage and set it up against the front of the house.

All so her grandmother could laugh at her killing herself.

"Seriously, Mik, don't get hurt," Skylar said. "Ladders freak me out."

"Good thing you're not on the ladder then, huh?" Mikaiya called from the fourth rung. She didn't need to go up all the way to knock the last of the autumn leaves out of her grandmother's gutters. *Gosh, how long have they been compacting up here?* Didn't one of the neighbors have a big enough heart to rush over and clean out Abby Marcott's gutters?

Nope! It was left up to Mikaiya, who used to impress her Portland neighbors with her handy skills. Apparently, growing up in a small town and spending her summers on a farm gave her skills most city folk never dreamed of acquiring.

People around here have the audacity to call me a city slicker... That should be reserved for Skylar, who still couldn't believe the grocery store closed at eight in the winters. She'd be shocked to know the summer hours only extended that until nine.

"On the other hand," Skylar said with a dreamy sigh, "I'm starting to see the appeal of having a butchy girlfriend. She can, like... do all the handiwork!"

Abby scoffed. "I thought *you* were her girlfriend."

"No. We're just friends."

"Then what the hell are you doing here?"

The rest of that weird conversation was drowned out when Mikaiya started knocking dense leaves out of the gutters. The scraping, the banging, and the cold fluttering of leaves to the ground created such a cacophony of sounds that Mik almost lost her hearing. Or maybe that was the crisp January air freezing her uncovered ears. She had remembered gloves, but her hat was still in her room. Who knew it would be colder up by the roof than on the ground? Wasn't hot air supposed to *rise?*

"Skylar's trying something new for a while," Mikaiya explained when her feet were on the grass again. A pile of slimy, crushed leaves were amassing beside the ladder, which meant she would be spending most of her afternoon cleaning it up with rakes and garbage bags. Trash collection already happened that day. Abby wouldn't mind if she had bags full of gross, dead leaves in her garage, right? "She's staying here until she gets a job and makes enough for her own place. Remember?" They had gone over this before Mik formally invited Skylar to come with her.

"Guess so," Abby mumbled.

"Sorry if I'm breaking your fantasies of having great-grandchildren with Mik," Skylar said with a giggle. "I'm sure she's working on that, though. Right, Mik?"

"What are you talking about?"

Skylar waved her off through the opened window. "You were right when you said small towns are built around mindless gossip. I can't go to the store without everyone stopping to ask me who I am and where I'm living! As soon as I drop your name, Mik, everyone starts asking me a million questions and telling me stories about you!"

The blood flowing in Mikaiya's veins came to a severe halt. "Excuse me?" she squeaked. "What are they saying?"

"Oh, that you're a lady killer. Some real heartbreaker."

Mikaiya turned away before Skylar could see the red burning in her cheeks. *Lady killer. Heartbreaker*. They must be talking about Ariana, the one who never left town and had wholly made this place her turf. *I'm so sorry, Ari*. Words Mik should have said ten years ago, but never had the balls to convey. When she finally had the words to explain herself, so much time had passed that she didn't see the point of dragging that up again. For all she knew, Ariana was with someone new. She had moved on, like Mik. Their foolish games as a couple of kids were a thing of the past. Now? God. It was happening all over again.

"You okay, Mik?"

Abby scoffed. "She's thinking about her ex."

Mikaiya couldn't swallow. Skylar had to do the talking for her.

"Oooh, which ex?"

"She used to date this girl back in high school. Really broke her heart, didn't you, Mik?"

Mikaiya finally swallowed that lump threatening to strangle her. "Sure did, Grandma. Suuuuure did." Ariana was now big enough to pound Mik's face in. *I would deserve it, too.* She bent down and gathered up the leaves into a neater pile. After rubbing her gloves against her jeans, she turned back to the ladder, determined to return to work.

Yet Skylar was so deep down the gossip drain that she wouldn't let it go. "She had a bit of a reputation back in Portland, too," she said to Abby, although loud enough for Mik to (unfortunately) hear. “She didn’t date much, but when she did, it always lasted like five minutes, and that was it!”

“Didn’t realize you were so knowledgeable about my dating life, Sky!” Mik called from the fifth rung.

“I think she’s got commitment issues,” Skylar said.

The last thing Mik heard was her grandmother saying, “You could say that!”

Geez, weren’t they getting cold with that open window? Wasn’t it time to close it and maybe leave poor Mikaiya alone? *I know I’m not innocent…* She picked debris out of the gutter and flecked it to the ground. *That was a long time ago.* Not like she killed somebody. She had been young and immature, but this business was between her and Ariana. *If everyone could shut up about it for two seconds, that would be great.* In a perfect world, nobody would know about what happened. Yet even if Ari hadn’t told a soul, word still would have discovered a way to get out. That’s how it always went. That was a big reason Mikaiya had to get the hell out of Paradise Valley when she had the chance. College had been that chance. So had been the summer job someone offered her the week of graduation.

She had never told Ari about it. What was the point, when Mik didn't decide to take her employer up on that offer until the moment she was handed her high school diploma? By then, fate had been spun. She knew what she had to do to protect her ass – and Ariana's.

The hardest part? Convincing herself it was the right thing to do. The reason Mikaiya never stayed in relationships for long – besides her busy job demanding more and more time out of her – was because deep down she was afraid of that night happening all over again.

She continued cleaning the gutters while thinking of Ari. The old her that Mik used to know. The new her that everyone in town was used to now. Mikaiya could never present her ex to Skylar and say, "*This is where it all began. Do you get it now?*" because the image Skylar would see was so far from what Mik used to see that there was no point. No chance of making Skylar see what it meant to hear the threats coming from another direction.

Eventually, it became easier to hop the ladder over bit by bit instead of racing up and down to move it. Like it became easier to think of the moments leading up to Mik's decision to stand the love of her young life up.

I wish you could understand, Ari. The ladder wobbled as Mikaiya took those little hops, one hand gripping the side while the other clung to Abby's sturdy gutters. *I didn't want to hurt you. I loved you! That's why I had to do it!*

Classic tale of misunderstandings with a violent undertone. Yet this wasn't the movies. Things wouldn't be neatly packaged up by the end of the week. Like there were no convenient coincidences to putting Mik on the path to patching things up with Ariana. Something she clearly had to do if she wanted to last five more minutes in her hometown.

She reached for the next glob of leaves still trapped in her grandmother's gutter. Two seconds later, the ladder was falling on its side, taking her down with it.

It was probably what she deserved.

Chapter 6

ARIANA

Brendon shoved his phone in Ariana's face. "Read this. Tell me I'm not a master wordsmith who is gonna change the world with his essays about..."

"I ain't readin' nothin'." Ariana shoved her sunglasses up her head, because it was better to tell him off using both of her big blue eyes than pretending she was a huge hotshot behind the glasses. "Don't you have anything better to do than sit on your ass and play on your phone?"

He shrugged. "Not really? We haven't had a call all day."

"Yeah, well, we might get one if you keep interrupting me." Ari turned back to her paperwork, set up in a clipboard that was as old as her. Heaven forbid anyone but her fill out the paperwork. Was Brendon literate? Sure, he wrote those weird essays about French philosophers and read books about renovating old European cathedrals, but that still didn't convince Ariana that Brendon knew what he was writing or thinking. This guy had too much of a death wish. Next, he would be ripping off his uniform and running down the rainy street wearing nothing but his underwear. He would claim it "revitalized his vitals," but would it make him late to the next call they inevitably received?

This was the part most EMTs hated about their shifts. The endless waiting. There was a reason the county only had a handful of full-time EMTs and paramedics, and it had nothing to do with budget. (All right, maybe a bit.) Little action came to towns like Paradise Valley, where Ariana spent most of her days. Sometimes she was back in Roundabout, but they had a smaller population that only saw an uptick of action during fireworks season. *Roundabout is where you go if you want to blow your arm off*. Ah, yes, hunting season as well. The only time Ari saw her fair share of bullet wounds was in the middle of autumn. And winter. And spring, and summer...

Basically, whenever the locals were bored enough to go out and shoot their guns.

The lull that day distressed her as well, but what could she do? While some EMTs approached work as, "*I'm paid to respond to calls, not wait for them,*" she wasn't the type to sit around and work on side projects or do homework until the calls came. She preferred to stay in the moment, either catching up on paperwork or training herself. Ideally, her coworkers would join her in the training so they would all remain sharp, but it was like herding cats some days. Like when Brendon kept draining his phone battery to read Kant.

Something isn't right today. Maybe it was the scent of rain coming in with the air. Or maybe it was that tamale she ate for lunch. *It was cooked all the way, right? I'm not getting salmonella from that chicken... I* better *not be getting salmonella...*

Her pencil was on its third flick against the clipboard when they got their call.

Ari tossed the paperwork over her shoulder while Brendon scrambled to get his seatbelt. Anything about his essay or what they might want to do for dinner went out the window as soon as the address came over the line.

"Whoo! I thought we were done with people falling down and hitting their heads!" Brendon braced himself against the door as Ariana turned on the siren and stepped on the gas. "You know I love me a good head injury!"

It wasn't until Ari turned at the four way stop that she realized where they were heading. "Oh, my God," she said, weaving between cars attempting to pull over for them. "It's Abby Marcott's house."

"You sure?"

"We were there a few months ago." Easy enough to remember an address like 4567 Colorado Street. Besides, Ari had been over there quite a bit when she was a kid. She always got a kick out of that address. "I wonder if she fell down."

"Well, they did say it was a female."

You mean like three fourths of this town? "Female" said nothing about who they could expect to see. Ari mentally prepared herself for seeing the feisty Abby Marcott down on her ass and struggling to remember who she was or where she was going. *We were the ones who responded to her 911 call after she realized she was having a stroke.* One of the major downsides of living in such a small town, let alone working in emergency services, was how many times she encountered people she grew up with, looked up to, and merely knew from passing by them on a daily basis. Seeing them with gaping wounds, frothing at the mouth, and turned upside down in their cars was not how she wanted to remember most of them. Except it was what she signed up for. It was what she had to face yet again.

Colorado Street was clear for that time of day. Ari maneuvered the ambulance into the empty driveway of Abby Marcott's house. She had completely forgotten about the existence of her ex-girlfriend – let alone the truck she had brought into town – until she leaped out of the driver's seat and found Abby hobbling toward her with a rickety walker.

Ari didn't hear what she said. She was too busy staring at Mik passed out on the ground, a ladder downed beside her.

You have got to be kidding me. Brendon jumped into action like the trained professional he was. Supposedly, Ari was *also* a train professional, but one would never guess from how she stood frozen a few feet away. For more than several seconds, she was the only one in the world who realized the irony of the situation. Everyone else, from Brendon the out of towner to Abby the grandmother who once fed Ari more than a few suppers, were too wrapped up in the emergency. If nothing else kicked Ari's ass and put her back to work, it was the worried look on Abby's face. Abigail Marcott did *not* look like that on a daily basis.

"Did you stabilize her head?" Ari asked her partner, who was already checking Mik's vitals while assuming that Ari prepared to move the patient from the scene. "How's her airways?"

It took a few more seconds for her to address the old woman standing by her walker and the younger woman too shocked to speak.

"When did this happen? Where did she fall from?"

Brendon announced that Mikaiya was breathing and that her head was stabilized. While they prepared to move her to the ambulance, Mik's eyes slowly fluttered open.

"Oh, Jesus..." she muttered. "What happened?"

"Mikkie!" Abby exclaimed, her hands death-gripping that walker as if she were about to fall down herself. "Are you okay? Can you hear me?"

Brendon held up his hand to silence the audience. By now, half of Colorado Street was peering from their windows and on their lawns taking in the scene. While Ari was used to having an audience while she did her work, she *wasn't* used to her ex-girlfriend being the patient in question. *The fuck do I do?* Her instincts wavered between the second nature that was her job, and the incessantly stewing anger she always felt in the pit of her stomach whenever she thought of Mikaiya Marcott. *In a perfect world, I could leave her here to rot. Honestly, a fall from a ladder couldn't have happened to a nicer person!*

Yet that wasn't the kind of vibe Ariana needed to invite into her life. She chose to follow the path that had been set by her training so many years before. *Someone is hurt or sick. I need to help them. That's my job.* It didn't matter if that person was the sweetest of girls next door, or the high school bully who all but ran Ariana off a road one night. There had been times when she treated people who were so surly, so offensively rude that she hesitated to believe that these were the same people thanking her for saving their lives later. *I'll never forget the day I treated one of the candidates for district representative for heat stroke. The one who basically said he hated gay people and wouldn't mind seeing us clear out of the area, although we make up a huge part of the economy here in Paradise Valley.* Yet none of those people compared to Mikaiya

Marcott, the one person in the world who would make Ari hesitate when treating them.

She was better than that. She had taken an oath to treat every patient with the same amount of respect, dignity, and care. Little Miss Heartbreaker shouldn't be any different.

Boy, this would be a riot later.

"Can you tell me your name?" Ariana shined a light into Mik's resistant eyes. *Maybe she got a nice concussion that she totally deserves. Doesn't mean I won't treat it.*

Mikaiya was so out of it that she probably didn't realize who hovered over her, anyway. "Mik... Mikai..."

"Do you know what year it is?"

"2018? No, wait..."

"Close enough," Brendon muttered. "I still think it's last year, too."

"How many fingers am I holding up?" Ari made a peace sign in front of her ex's face. For a single second, she remembered when they couldn't take a single selfie without putting bunny ears behind each other's heads. Typical teen stuff. How long ago it seemed.

"Two?"

"I don't think she has a concussion," Ariana said. "Or at least she didn't hit her head *that* hard."

"Still gotta make sure she didn't hurt her neck or spine."

"Yup."

After estimating the length of the fall and how Mik landed, Ariana figured that the proper precautions should be enough to ensure Mikaiya healed well enough. They were still taking her the hospital for more thorough examinations. Too bad that meant putting her hands on Mik for a few seconds to safely transport her into the back of the ambulance.

"We're taking her to county," Brendon announced. "She'll be fine, but if you want to meet us there, I'm sure she'll appreciate it."

The out-of-towner, with her "ironic" T-shirt, high-waisted pants, and hair up in a bun, almost offered to ride with Mikaiya. Yet she suddenly remembered Abby's presence and announced she would drive them both to the hospital... could anyone tell her where it was?

"You ride with her," Ariana said to her partner. "I'll drive."

"Naturally," Brendon said with a shrug. Ari was already driving that day. Her getting behind the wheel again probably didn't seem out of the ordinary. *Yet I would be driving, whether he liked it or not.* The thought of riding in the back of the ambulance with her ex-girlfriend was more horrifying than giving her mouth to mouth. Mikaiya was coming more and more into consciousness. The last thing they needed was another conversation in forced proximity.

Abby gave Ari a critical look as they parted ways. Once Ariana was behind the wheel and buckled up, she turned on the siren and got them the hell out of there. Although Mik was technically only a few feet away, hitting that gas pedal made Ariana feel like she put considerable distance between herself and the feelings gnawing away at her bones and sinew.

It still wasn't far enough.

Chapter 7

MIKAIYA

Staying in the county hospital, where she had been born and suffered the brunt of her softball injuries, was not how Mikaiya planned to spend her weekend. Nor did she think she'd be seeing the inside of the hospital that first month back in Paradise Valley. Not unless her grandmother became sick again.

Instead of sitting by her grandmother's beside, however, it was Abby sitting next to Mik's.

"Hasn't the food quality gone absolutely down in the past twenty years?" Abby asked, as if Mik could remember what hospital food tasted like when she was eight. “I felt like I was eating ass instead of oatmeal when I stayed here. It’s tragic! What are they charging us for?”

Mikaiya shrugged. *Feels pretty nice to no longer wear a neck brace.* That had been her first day of hell, when she struggled to stay conscious, no matter how often the doctors and nurses asked her inane question and snapped their fingers to get her attention. She was assured that sleepiness was normal, but that didn’t mean she should always “give into temptation,” as they put it. They were on the fence about whether she had a concussion, but by the end of that first day, hands were thrown into the air and “fuck its” shared among the hospital staff.

Still, they wanted to keep her overnight for observation. By noon on Friday, Mikaiya was unceremoniously sent home in her grandmother’s truck, which she was not allowed to drive. Neither was Abby, who still had motor troubles from her stroke. It was left to Skylar to take a crash course in stick shifts. Again. Because she had somehow managed to get her and Abby to the hospital and back on Thursday, but she acted like she had never done it before by the time Mikaiya was back in the passenger seat.

"I swear to God, Sky," Mikaiya mumbled as they started and stopped their way out of the hospital parking lot. "If you kill me on the way home from the hospital, you're going to a special kind of hell."

"Sorry, Mik! They didn't teach us this in driving school! Everything is automatic there!"

"Yet you *somehow* managed to get to the hospital!"

"It took me two hours."

"It's a twenty-seven mile drive!"

Skylar chuckled as she finally found her stride on the road. "I see the fall didn't hurt your sense of righteous indignation."

Mik scoffed. "Did you hear that I'm not supposed to drive for a whole week? I'm supposed to get a checkup in town that day, so I guess you better get used to driving stick."

"I'm sure there's a straight girl joke in there somewhere."

Although she wanted to laugh, the best Mikaiya could do was lean her head back and close her eyes before the jerking scenery made her nauseas. She couldn't bring herself to make the obvious jokes about heterosexual Skylar failing to "drive stick" and that it probably meant she was destined to become a full-time citizen of Paradise Valley for all the wrong reasons.

"By the way," Mik said, changing the subject. "Do you remember what EMTs came to help me? I barely remember anything from that moment."

Skylar shrugged. "Beats me. I don't know the townspeople like you do. Seemed like they did a great job making sure you were stable before hauling you off."

Groaning, Mikaiya continued, "Was one of them a woman?"

"Guess so. At least one of them was a guy."

"You're so helpful."

"What do you want from me? I was freaking out a bit yesterday. Didn't really take any time to see what the EMTs were packing in their shirts and pants. Why do you care, anyway? You got some bad blood with one of the EMTs in town and think they were going to half-ass it on you?"

Mikaiya blushed. "You might say that."

"Geez. I'm sure glad I'm not from around here. Sounds like drama lasts for decades."

"It does if you really fucked up."

Skylar was silent for a moment. Instead of struggling to change gears, however, she glanced in her friend's direction and asked, "Did you really fuck up, Mik?"

"Yup."

Silence filled the cab of the old, rusty truck for more than a few seconds. "You gonna tell me how you fucked up?"

"Do I have to? You're the one person in town who doesn't hate my guts, probably."

"Jesus, what did you do? Run over the mayor's dog?"

"Not quite. Remember when my grandmother told you that I broke my ex's heart when I moved to Portland?" She didn't offer any further explanation than that.

"Uh huh." Skylar could hardly keep her eyes on the road. Good thing there wasn't anyone else around that time of day. "What about it?"

A sigh broke the next ensuing silence. Mikaiya might as well get this off her chest. Skylar was going to hear it around town sooner rather than later, and she should hear it straight from one of the original sources. Otherwise, she'd get the Anem Singer special when buying her tampons and canned green beans. "Yeah, so, turns out that my ex is now one of the full-time EMTs in this town. She was actually the gal who talked to us that first night, when we found that wreck blocking the road."

Skylar was reverently quiet while she digested that information. "That was a *woman?*"

"C'mon, Sky."

"I kid, I kid. A little." Skylar cleared her throat. "Well, that's awkward."

"No kidding. I haven't been in town for two weeks, and not only do I fall on my freakin' head, but Ari was probably called to come knock some sense back into me."

"Ari?"

"Her full name is Ariana, but everyone calls her Ari." *Especially now*. Mik couldn't imagine that fantastic example of all things gloriously butch going by *Ariana*.

"Like the singer?"

"Yeah. Like the singer." Another reason Ari probably wasn't going by Ariana anymore. "She wasn't always butch, though. We actually had a pretty traditional butch-femme relationship back in high school." She stole a look in Skylar's direction. "I was the butch, in case there's any confusion."

"I'm not gonna pretend to know what that all entails. Didn't exactly see that kind of stuff in my high school."

"It was different at our school." Clark High was far from the bastion of progressive values Skylar may now associate it with, but when over half the students at least came from LGBT-dominant families, it wasn't unusual for queer kids to feel more comfortable coming out and emulating the relationships they saw at home. Abby had called her granddaughter's relationship with Ariana "quaint," because they reminded Mrs. Marcott of what the local bar scene had looked like when she first moved to Paradise Valley. That had also changed a lot in the past decade. Mik had witnessed it in Portland as well. While it didn't affect her perception as much, it became most jarring when she saw someone like Ariana walking around town. Was that really the same girl who once put her hair in a big, frizzy braid and did cartwheels on the farm for Mik's amusement? *I used to get such a kick from seeing her underwear under her skirts.* Was it really only ten years ago? That amount of time meant nothing to the average adult, but ten years ago had still been Mikaiya's teenaged years. Time was slower back then. Everything was big, *major,* the worst and best thing to ever happen. Mik didn't doubt that the night she stood Ariana up was etched in their brains, forever.

God knew Mik had been thinking about it more since coming back to town.

"So your ex-girlfriend, whom you dumped like a real champ, now has one of the most important jobs in your small town. It's probably safe to say that most of the townsfolk are more sympathetic toward her than, say, the girl who ran out and didn't come back until she really had to?"

Mikaiya grimaced.

"Uh huh. Good luck with that, Mik. Hope I'm also not guilty by association."

"You're guiltier of being an outsider. At least I have native clout around these parts." In a small town, that was the most important thing, hands *down*.

"Yeah, well, that 'native clout' might not mean much if everyone is pissed at you, Mik. No wonder you never want to leave the house. I thought you hated the lack of anonymity around here. Now I know you get extra doses of judgment every time you pick up milk from the grocery store."

At least I'm not getting it from Anem. God, would Anem Singer be the extent of Mikaiya's dating pool if she decided to get back into the local game? Some people would always look up to her and admire her, even if they should have known better. All the good it did Mik. Anem wasn't really her type. Maybe back in high school, when Mikaiya had a heart that beat for soft curves and pretty smiles beneath a cloud of fuzzy hair. But growing up had taught Mik a few things about her tastes. Perhaps she wasn't afraid of facing Ariana again because she assumed her ex would be as demure as ever.

"I've gotta talk to her," she mumbled, hoping that Skylar hadn't heard her. *I need to at least explain what happened. After I'm done thanking her for saving my life, I guess.* Who knew if Mikaiya's life was actually in any danger after that fall? Not like she had plummeted more than ten feet. Still, it could've gone much differently had she landed a different way. In that case, she was more than grateful that Ariana set aside any animosity between them in the name of helping someone in need.

Apparently, however, Skylar had heard her. "Not like it's hard to find people in a small town, Mik. I've had more of the same people saying hello to me every day than I ever did back in Portland, and you know me, I always ran the same route. You'd think that old guy who always sat on the corner of Division and Sixteenth would have at least said hi..."

"You have a point." Mikaiya wouldn't have to go out of her way to find Ariana. Odds were high that she'd step out of her childhood home and encounter the intimidating EMT on her way to the farmer's market. *I wonder what she does when she's not working...* Where did she live? Did she have a significant other? She probably assumed that Skylar was Mik's girlfriend, but that couldn't be further from the truth. They were equal parts single, just looking for different kinds of people to love.

I haven't really loved anyone since you, Ari. Everyone knew how heartbroken Ariana had been when they broke up. But did they know how much Mikaiya cried, and how she almost sabotaged her first semester of college by refusing to get out of bed and doing her damn homework? Ariana wasn't the only one dealing with raw, open wounds. Although Mik wouldn't argue that her ex definitely had the shock value on top of everything else.

Mikaiya was old enough and a little bit wiser now to realize how she screwed up that long-ago night. The way she handled it? Immaturity at its finest. Eighteen-year-old Mikaiya thought she was doing the right thing by taking off in the middle of the night with no word to anyone, least of all the girl who thought she was going with her. Getting out of town was of the utmost importance, however. The more distance she put between herself and her girlfriend? The less likely the shit was about to hit the fan.

They had been kids. Back then, Mikaiya only understood the concept of running the hell away from the dangers lurking in every corner. There were no consequences. Only getting the hell out of Dodge before the grim reaper brought his threats to life.

A shudder ripped through Mikaiya. That was the kind of flashback she did not need so soon after falling on her head.

"Tell you what, Mik," Skylar said. "I've got the couch all made up for you at home. I've been so frazzled since your fall yesterday that I've totally abandoned my job search. I need to get back to it. So how about we hang out in your grandma's living room and watch some Netflix? No chill." She flashed Mikaiya a smile. "Only because you're in such a delicate position. Also, I've been meaning to rewatch the last season of '*Orange is the New Black.*' You can help fill me in on some things. Make sure your head is working right."

Mikaiya rolled her eyes. She didn't know if it was the bump on her head or the bad memories tracing their paths down the bridge of her nose that made such a simple act hurt so much.

Chapter 8

ARIANA

"Sometimes I want to write him a letter," Frankie Nicolauer, the owner and operator of the eponymous Frankie's Deli smacked the giant hardcover copy of *It* against her thigh. "Ask him if he's ever thought about making an official Cliff's Note version of this book. Because I swear to God I have not slogged through a book this badly since *IQ84*."

A few snickers went around the circle. Ariana looked up from the notes she had scribbled into the composition notebook she used strictly for the biweekly book club at the library. Paradise Valley Public Library loved to tote that they hosted the "biggest" Stephen King book club in Oregon, although that had yet to be proven. Looking around the table in the meeting room, Ari wasn't sure how true it was. Only six people had shown up that week, although it was better than the three that sometimes cropped up around Christmastime. Ari rarely missed a meeting. Ever since she drowned her misery in *Carrie* back when she was nursing that broken heart, she had seen Mr. King as the master of all literature. Didn't matter if she read books she technically liked better, or if he put out a dud that had her scratching her head. Most often, his books were the only ones she made time to read… like when waiting for a call at work. She often gave her coworkers a hard time for not using their downtime wisely, but there she often was, sneaking pages of *The Shining* when nobody else was looking.

One of the first things she had written about *It,* from both memory and from this recent reread, was that she loved how "meaty" it was. Ari was the kind of woman who liked to get lost in her nighttime reads. She liked knowing that there was still plenty of book left to go. Nothing was worse than finishing a book and having nothing to follow it that night. Over the years, Ari had slowly amassed her own hardbound collection of King's books, but she still often relied on the library, which only had a limited amount of copies for the monthly reads. She didn't have to worry about *It,* however. That was one of the first books she purchased at the used book store in Cannon Beach, back when she attended an EMT training camp in the area.

"I like how long the book is," Ari said after the laughter had died.

Book club leader Hesper Chess, also known as everyone's favorite due-diligence accountant, cleared her throat. "Why don't we talk about the lines we've underlined this month? Kendra, you always have some good ones."

Kendra was too busy doodling another rough sketch in her notebook to pay much attention. "Huh?" she said, looking up from what would surely be the next big piece to go into her gallery. "Um..."

When an uncomfortable silence befell the small group, Ariana looked at her lines, hoping to find something worthy of sharing. Yet for a woman who wasn't afraid to cough up her opinions, she still struggled to read aloud, like she was back in high school and unable to get through a single page of *The Scarlet Letter,* while the class snickered around her. Her reading abilities had improved greatly since her early twenties, but she was still self-conscious when reading simple lines she pulled out of a book. It didn't help that she probably pulled one of the most well-known quotes. Because if there was one thing Ari related to in a book like this one, it had to be a young boy's crush on another girl.

"I like the poem Ben wrote about Bev," she eventually offered to the group. "It's one of them haikus." At least she remembered that from high school English class.

"Yes, it is," Hesper said. "Do you have it available to read for the rest of us?"

"I'd rather not, if it's okay." Ariana hated that she accompanied that with one of her nervous tics, also known as the ol' scratching the top of her scalp. "*People will think you have lice again if you're always doing that!*" her mother once admonished. Mom wasn't around any longer, but the warning remained every time Ari scratched her head. "You know how I am about reading out loud."

"I think most of us are familiar with it," Padmini Singh, from the antique shop, said. "You can't scroll for two seconds on Goodreads without seeing someone share it like they're suddenly the most well-read person in town."

Hesper cleared her throat. She was always the prim and proper conductor of this association when given the chance, and boy, did they give her the chance *now*. The way she straightened her wire-rimmed glasses and adjusted her Harry Potter-themed scarf around her neck was almost adorable. Too bad Ariana never had the balls to ask her out. *She doesn't go for women like me.* Ari didn't go for women who had the potential to make her feel stupid, whether they realized it or not. Her mild attraction to Hesper was purely aesthetical.

"What do you like about the poem, Ari?"

"Well, ah…" This time it was Ariana clearing her throat. "It's a good poem, you know?" Yeah. That sounded super intelligent. Right up there with her winning literary analyses in high school. "I really like the part about Bev's hair being like 'January embers.' At first it's really literal, 'cause she has red hair, but when you dig into the description, you realize he picked January for a reason."

Everyone around the table gave her a quizzical look. Great. She had to pull more words out of her ass?

"We don't associate January with heat, but when you have a nice fire on the coldest nights of the year, you really appreciate it. Bev's hair is this heat that he is responding to. Bringing him out of the cold." Ari scratched her head again. "That's all I've got."

Everyone but Kendra nodded. She wrinkled her nose before going back to her doodling.

That's not the only reason I like that poem. King could've called it a fire, a blaze, or a wildfire. Embers was intentional. It had to be.

Because embers were the remnant of that passionate fire burning in someone's heart. Embers meant the fire had quelled, but could easily be stoked back to life with a hand that knew what it was doing. How many times had Ari lit a fire, left the bozos she lived with to keep it alive, and returned to find it almost nothing but ash? All it took was another log, a little stoking, and boom. Fire for another few hours.

It was a lot like love. Fires couldn't simply be left to blaze. They had to be tended. Someone had to watch it. Couldn't let it get too crazy or destructive... but also couldn't let it burn out because nobody was there to keep it alive.

Then again, she really liked the word *ember,* and that was all there was to it.

Ariana kept her mouth shut until the end of the meeting, when Hesper asked them to count votes for February's pick. Thinking about Mikaiya made Ari suggest *Carrie,* but she was overruled when Kendra glibly suggested the first book of *The Dark Tower*. Everyone who didn't groan empathically put up their hands to vote for it.

"See you in two weeks?" Hesper asked Ari when most of the group was gone. "By the way, I really liked your contribution with the poem."

If Ariana weren't so rattled by her ex's reappearance, she would suggest they go over to Heaven's Café and get a drink to talk more about it. *Yeah, that would be smooth. Way too smooth for me.* Even after so much change, Ari still preferred to have women ask her out instead of the other way around. She liked the validation it gave her, although that wasn't always the healthiest approach. Still, Hesper wasn't the kind of gal who went around town asking people out. She was more reserved than the typical librarian (and Paradise Valley's librarian was *far* from typical,) and Ari wasn't sure she dated. Hell, was she gay?

"Thanks." That was all she said before turning toward the door. "I plan on being here in two weeks. See you." Maybe in two weeks she would have the fortitude to ask Hesper out for coffee. Not even on a date. For *coffee.*

Probably not, however. Because the first thing Ariana saw when she emerged from the meeting room was a familiar face that hit her like a truck.

There Mikaiya was, browsing the New to Paradise Valley shelves toward the front of the library. Her finger was on a donated copy of *A Wrinkle in Time*. Was that a coincidence? Or did she not recall borrowing Ari's whole collection when they first started hanging out all those years ago? Ariana no longer owned those books. They had gone into the ether with most of her childhood possessions. Kinda like how she thought of Mikaiya sometimes.

What should she do? Sneak out? Hold back and wait for Mikaiya to leave? The first one was nearly impossible since there was only one exit, and Mik was right next to it. The other option meant hiding out in the meeting room and hoping there was no one using it soon. Even if Ari chose that option, she risked Mik seeing her through the windows. Nothing private happened in that library. It was a miracle that the bathroom stalls didn't have windows, too.

"Hell," she muttered, her bookbag slipping down her arm. Never before had a Stephen

King book weighed so damn much. *What's your problem? She's only your ex. She doesn't run this town. Neither do you, but at least everyone likes you well enough. Get over there and act like a mature adult. If you can.*

It didn't help that Ari kept staring at Mik's ass. Those skinny jeans sure did look good on her. For a woman who didn't do anything super athletic anymore – that Ari knew of, anyway – Mikaiya still had a nice ass and semi-muscular legs. Maybe she was a runner. Jessie Main would love to have a running buddy when she wasn't training on her bicycle. *Probably would like to screw her brains out, too.*

Why did Ari narrow her eyes when she thought that? What was that weird sensation stirring in her gut again?

Jealousy? Fuck, no!

Ariana Mura was *not* jealous over the thought of Mikaiya *Marcott* of all people flirting with, dating, and making merry with other women. Why would she be? This was the stupid git who broke her heart two years ago! The one who came crawling back into town without a warning to anyone. Or at least, with no warning to Ariana, the one woman who needed a warning more than anyone else.

What did she care if she went on to break someone else's heart? Not like most of the townspeople didn't know that "something" happened between them. Even the newbies knew that Abby Marcott's granddaughter had broken Ari's heart. Like everyone knew that Ariana used to be a very different person back in high school. *Was I really, though? Maybe I'm not so different, after all.* What was the point of dressing up the fireplace in a new façade when the same embers from ten years ago quietly cooled deep inside?

Shame overcame Ariana for a single second. Shame that she might still have unfinished feelings for Mik. Shame that she was clearly attracted to a poem in some random book because it reminded her of those simmering feelings that never really went away. *I said so myself. The more you stoke a fire, the more it burns.* Ari had always harbored little embers of love and passion for the girl who stomped on her heart without a single explanation. With Mik gone, however, there was no one standing around tending that fire slowly burning out in Ari's chest.

Mikaiya was back in town, though. Did that mean the fire was coming back to life?

No. No, no, no!

Ari would prove it, too. She'd march out there and act like nothing was up between them. Mik hadn't noticed her yet, anyway. Ariana totally had the element of surprise. If Mik *did* see her and decided to do something about it, Ari could play it cool. It was a small town. The last thing Ariana wanted was witnesses – like the librarian on duty - who could say that she saw the two of them freaking each other out like it was prom all over again.

With her head held high, Ariana sauntered through the library, past the recent acquisitions shelf, and straight toward the door. She should be in her truck within ten seconds. She always got the best parking spot – the one at the far end of the lot, beneath the shade of an oak tree.

"Ari!"

So much for the element of surprise. The moment that voice hit her in the back of the head, Ariana froze like a deer trapped in her own truck's headlights.

God damnit, what do I do? While Mik didn't *bound* out from behind the bookshelf, she was quick to be within Ariana's line of sight. *I can't blow her off.* That could result in a scene that librarian patrons were more than excited to gossip about at the grocery store and in the post office. Ari could hear it now. She'd step into line to mail off a package, and she'd hear half of Paradise Valley whispering and giggling over her presence.

Yet the thought of facing Mikaiya for some pleasant conversation was so far from possibility that Ariana was probably better off jetting out of the library and revving her truck until it took her far, far away.

"Hey."

Smooth. Really smooth. Ariana had not only acknowledged the ex she was about to coolly walk by, but she had more or less invited her into conversation. *Be real. You only want an excuse to stare at her.* Mik was dressed down in jeans and a baggy green flannel shirt – real flannel, not that sheer shit city girls got in boutiques. Her hair wasn't as finely combed as it had been the last few times they encountered one another, and there wasn't a spot of makeup on her face. *No concealer, either. Jesus, that's a whopper of a pimple.* Being back in town did that to a woman, though. Who the hell cared about appearances when everyone knew what you looked like when you were a kid wearing diapers, anyway?

Whatever shock had been on Mik's face slowly faded away as she realized it was her turn to speak. Or, Ariana presumed, it was *her* chance to get away.

Yet she kept standing there, as if she expected a formal apology.

"I wanted to thank you." Well, that worked, too. Mikaiya awkwardly rubbed her arm, the baggy flannel calling attention to the fact she still kept her body in shape. She wasn't anywhere near as strong as Ariana anymore, but compared to her, Mik had barely undergone the same transformation as her ex. Age and maturity had done a small number, but she was still undeniably *Mikaiya,* the girl with a killer throwing arm and a smile that could get her a date if she played her cards right down at the bar. (Because in Paradise Valley, *every* bar was a de facto gay bar.) "I hear that you were one of the EMTs who came when I fell off that ladder the other day."

"Yeah, uh..." Ariana sniffed up the courage to say something, anything that might come across as semi-intelligent and totally not related to their past drama. "Wasn't that only days ago? I didn't know you were out of the hospital." That much was true.

"Doctors didn't think there was anything wrong with me. Only a nice bump on my head that's a little sore." Mik continued to rub her arm. Did she know she was so nervous? Was this Ariana's chance to say something witty on her way out the door? *Yes*. Would she take the chance to drop the mic and march out of the library like the eternal badass she wanted to believe she was? *No*. Her throat was dry.

Probably from that tiny wisp of smoke rising from the embers still simmering in her heart.

"You should still be careful. Sometimes it's hard to detect a concussion if you don't have any obvious symptoms."

"Thanks. I'll keep that in mind." Mik offered a smile that *may* have been genuine, but Ari was so conditioned to be wary around her ex that she didn't know what to make of those pearly whites flashing in her direction. "I've been taking it easy. Doctor said not to drive for a week, but nothing about going for a walk. I needed some stuff to read, anyway. I saw something about a Stephen King book club today."

Ari's eyes widened. *Don't you dare.* Who did she mentally address that to? Mik the interloper? Or herself? Don't what? Dare to invite her to book club? That wouldn't be obvious at all. "Yeah, a few of us gather a couple times a month to read a King book. This month's is *It.* Everyone got a hankering to read it after the movie came to town."

"I didn't know you were a Stephen King fan."

Ariana tried not to wince. “Recent development. That said, I wouldn’t suggest you check out any of his books right now. They tend to be out all the time. Word gets around about a good read, you know.”

“I see.” Mik turned forty-five degrees, as if she were about to grab a book off the new arrivals’ shelf. “Actually, there was something else I wanted to ask you.”

If there were conversations going on around them, Ariana no longer heard them. She barely heard the blood pumping in and out of her heart. *Am I supposed to hear that?* She was an EMT. Shouldn’t she know? “Uh, what?” Although Ariana spoke at her normal volume, she swore her voice boomed across the library, summoning any and all attention to be had. “If it’s about your head, you should ask a doctor. I’m simply an EMT. Not even a paramedic.”

“No, it’s not about that.”

“All right.”

Mikaiya cocked her head. Bemusement? Trepidation? Both swarmed her heart-shaped face that had thinned out since high school. Ari didn't know it was possible for her to look cuter than she did back then. *I wonder what that makes me now.* Ariana clamped her lips together before she said something stupid.

"I was wondering if you and I might have a private chat sometime soon." What gave? Mik could lower her voice and *not* have everyone in the library look in their direction? She actually kept it at a decent volume? Feh. That wasn't fair. Ari swore she couldn't breathe right now without alarming God up in Heaven. "I think we have some things to talk about if I'm going to be back in town."

Not that Ari was in the business of smiling at people, but she surprised herself when she knitted her brows into a scowl and frowned so hard she swore she smelled something foul. *It's all the bullshit coming out of this one's mouth.* "I don't know what there is to talk about. You're back in town. So what? Just stop falling off ladders. It's not good for you." *And it makes me have to come see you.* Bad enough Ari saw her ex all around town now, after ten years of blissful separation.

All right, so it wasn't always so blissful. Especially that year after she was dumped. The only reason it didn't extend to two years was because Ari finally threw herself into something productive. She wouldn't say she became an EMT *because* of Mik, but that breakup and subsequent time apart certainly allowed Ariana to figure herself out and grow up a little.

More like a lot...

"Well," Mikaiya squeaked, "we didn't really get a lot of closure, and..."

"We've both moved on," Ari hissed. "I've got my life, you've got yours. You don't seem to be held too far back from relationships. I saw how much your new girl cares about you when I had to come bail you out of an injured neck."

Mikaiya truly embraced bemusement now. "My 'new girl?' Oh, you mean Skylar?" She laughed, as if that were the most ridiculous thing anyone in town had said to her since she got back. "She's not my girlfriend. Just a friend. For shit's sake, she's straight."

Ari took a step back. "Then what is she doing *here?*"

"I know, right? She followed me here from Portland. Said she wanted out of that city life, so... here she is, looking for a job in a town where it's all about who you know."

Ariana scoffed. "You know what? Fine. Let's talk." Before Mik could smile in relief, Ari continued, "but not today. I've got shit to do." That shit included decompressing from this run-in. Ari needed a beer and a TV show to take her mind off things. "I have Tuesday off. I assume you don't have much going on around here and that day will work for you." Maybe give her a little time to realize she really did have a graver head injury after all. Couldn't hang out if she was trapped in bed with trauma!

"You're right about that." Mikaiya pulled out her phone and opened her calendar. Everything was clear. Ari didn't know if she was more impressed with that, or the fact that Mik's phone was so big other people could *see* what it said. "I'm free Tuesday. All I do is catch up on my grandma's chores and make sure she doesn't overextend herself." She sighed. "Where should we meet? Heaven's?"

"No. We're going for a light hike up Wolf's Hill. Just the two of us." That way nobody could hear their screams. Of anger. At each other. That were inevitable. *I'm not going to kill her, I swear!* "Unless it turns out you really do have a concussion, in which case we shall reschedule." Ariana may be trained to handle it, but she wasn't about to volunteer her life-saving services unless it was necessary.

Mikaiya let out a low whistle before lowering both arms, knuckles pressing into her hips. The movement opened the front of her flannel, revealing a tight V-neck beneath it. *Great! Nice cleavage! See that hasn't changed!* "A hike, huh? You want to torture me? Well, I probably deserve that. Fine! Weather permitting, we'll meet in the parking lot at the base of Wolf's Hill." Mik turned around as if she were about to leave. At the last second, she turned back around. "What time? Should I bring lunch?"

Ari slowly shook her head. "Eat a big breakfast. I'll see you at eleven on Tuesday."

They parted ways soon after. Mik headed toward the bathrooms, and Ariana continued her march outside. She shot the librarian on duty a warning-filled look that what happened here should *not* be passed around town. Whether it did any good... well, she'd find out the following day, now wouldn't she?

By then, the regret would settle in as well. Yet her pride refused to let her cancel. Although when Tuesday rolled around, she was compelled to stand her ex up at the base of Wolf's Hill. *See how she likes it.*

Which was exactly why she got in her truck at 10:30. Yup.

Chapter 9

MIKAIYA

She shut off the engine and let out a giant, resolved sigh. The silence brought into the cab of her truck reminded Mik that she was out in the middle of nowhere, among the trees, the brush, and the open sky – that was currently covered in thick, graying clouds. Kinda smelled like rain. Good thing Mikaiya brought her rain jacket and a hat with a small visor. She may be a native Oregonian, but there was still nothing worse than water in her face.

Well, clearly I'm well enough to drive. That was the one positive of this moment she'd take to bed with her that night. It wasn't quite one week since her fall, and the doctor had been pretty clear that she not drive by herself. Yet here she was, sitting alone in her truck at the base of Wolf's Hill two miles out of town. She had snuck out of her grandmother's house right after breakfast, around the same time when Skylar rushed out to a last-minute job interview at the GP's clinic. It was Mikaiya's chance. Not that she had considered standing her ex up. All right, so maybe the thought had passed her mind… but only as a self-defense mechanism. The thought of marching up one of the biggest landmarks in the county with the ex she had wronged made Mik so woozy that she almost wondered if she had a concussion, after all.

She glanced to the side and saw Ariana's truck parked at the far side of the public lot. There was only one other truck around, and it was surrounded by young men in their hiking gear. Looked like they were finished for the day. Either that, or they were simply psyching themselves up for another round up and down the hill.

Where the hell was Ari, though? She hadn't gone ahead of Mik, had she?

Maybe the wolves got her. Wolf's Hill was named after a small rock formation near the summit. Someone had decided it looked like a wolf howling at the moon, and the name stuck. Yet there used to be more than a few wolves in the area, too. Back before they ran away from encroaching civilization or were hunted down by ranchers protecting their livestock. Now it was a rarity to see a wolf. Coyotes were more common, since so many of the ones in the area had little fear of humans. Same with the raccoons. Two of them had come by the house the other night to root through the garbage, and poor Skylar was not prepared for huge hissing "trash pandas" with claws the size of her face. That was the same day they found out the neighbor's cat had been killed. *Raccoons don't play the hell around. Neither do coyotes.*

Wolves, though. They were more cautious around humans, but that may have only spoken to their intelligence. *Ari always reminded me of a wolf, even before her big transformation.*

Only back in high school, Mik was more likely to call her a wily little fox. She had definitely grown into a wolf, though. A big, silently tough one that was as likely to rip out her throat as she was to calmly walk away, living to fight another day.

"You gonna get out of that truck or what?"

Mik almost jumped out of her seat. There, beside the passenger-side window, was Ariana dressed in a slim black rain jacket and a scarf that could easily be wrapped around her head should it start raining. Then again, she was probably a woman who was used to traipsing about in the natural elements. An EMT couldn't control the weather when it came to responding to calls.

"Good morning to you, too." Mikaiya unsnapped her seatbelt and opened her door. Ariana remained on the other side. "Great weather, huh?"

"For January, it's not so bad. At least it's not freezing."

No. Mik supposed it wasn't. Nothing like the freezes they had the past couple of years, particularly around Portland. Not a bit of snow, and the only ice on the roads came in the dead of night when it maaaaybe reached sub-thirty degrees. It was always melted by the time most of the world woke up.

They reconvened at the start of the well-worn trail. “I haven’t climbed this hill since high school,” Mikaiya said, almost forgetting who she was talking to. *You know, when we used to steal up here for some alone time?* Ariana wasn’t the only one Mik went hiking with, though. Abby Marcott used to be a lot spryer back in the day. Hell, anyone with two working ankles and decent joints took the slow trails up the gentle hill. The reason it was so popular was because almost anyone could reach the summit in about an hour. In the summer, it was covered in sunshine, greenery, and that touch of fauna that made both the locals and the tourists swoon. In January, however, it was simply a common place to stretch one’s legs, as long as they didn’t mind getting a little wet.

“I figured it would give us some privacy,” Ariana said.

Mik was slightly taken aback. "Yeah. Good idea." She didn't delude herself into thinking they were randy teenagers looking for a pretty place to make out – and maybe more. Mik shuddered. *We were really dumb back then.* It hadn't been enough to hold hands and steal kisses. They had to get dirty against old trees and in the tall, ant-infested grass. Always sounded romantic in their heads, but Mikaiya hated having to explain all the bug bites in the most unnatural of places. Luckily, her grandmother never asked many questions.

We have things to talk about… Mik had been rehearsing what she wanted to say for the past few days. How *did* one explain the terrible circumstances behind what may have been the worst night of their lives?

They spent the first part of the ascent awkwardly talking about their families. Mik was surprised to hear that Ariana no longer had much contact with what was left of her family in Roundabout. It had nothing to do with her sexuality, and everything to do with a house fire that destroyed many of their possessions. *I had no idea...* That was something Abby had never told her granddaughter during their monthly phone calls. Mik heard all about the businesses that came and went from Paradise Valley, but not the minutiae of who moved out and whose houses burned down.

"At least nobody died?" Mik said, feet attempting to trip over a straight portion of the trail. Ari looked back at her as if she had done that on purpose. "Sorry about some of your childhood stuff, though."

"Nobody died, but it was a good excuse to put a lot of things behind me." Ari shrugged. "The person I was then, and the person I am now are completely different."

Mikaiya momentarily stopped, allowing Ari to get a few more paces ahead of her. Some rain fell through the canopy rising above them. Dirt slowly turned back into mud. Not enough to make their ascent too dangerous, but enough that Mik took note of it. *Glad I wore my best boots.* They didn't get much use in Portland, but she had already broken them in after two weeks back in Paradise Valley.

"I'm pretty different, too," Mik finally said. "I've grown up a lot since high school. I guess Portland helped a lot with that." She didn't expand on what that meant, because she doubted Ariana would be impressed with the details. But going to college and getting a job in Portland's biggest city had definitely matured her and hardened both her external and internal shells. People came and went so easily in Portland, a city that had become as transient as other worldly American hubs. She had been exposed to cultures she only read about in high school textbooks. The poverty and crime exhibited in certain pockets (that grew the longer she stayed there) toughened her up to a world that wasn't as kind as she wanted to believe it was. The hustle and bustle of city life gave her that rush of energy she had always craved while growing up in a small, rural town, but it also exposed her to anxieties she never knew existed. People said she didn't look too different from her high school days, but she felt different. That was what made coming back to Paradise Valley so hard.

I'm not the person you used to know, Ari. Like I hardly know you anymore. This well-built woman sauntering up the gentle slope of Wolf's Hill was so different from the stringy girl who used to giggle against Mikaiya's lips, that Mik barely knew who she was!

"Guess that fancy job wasn't all it was cracked up to be, huh?" Ari asked over her shoulder.

After the first drop hit her scalp, Mikaiya pulled on her hat. "What did you hear about it?"

"Only that after you graduated, you got some job in marketing. Don't know what for, or who it was about, only that it was 'marketing.'"

"Well, it's true. I worked for a marketing firm headquartered in downtown Portland. They said I was one of the lucky ones, because out of everyone in my PSU program, I was the one selected to come work for them a few months after graduation." She didn't mention that she used those few months to backpack around Europe with a girl she couldn't stop fooling around with for more than a few seconds. That relationship had been doomed before it began, but the backpacking trip extended its life a few precious breaths. As soon as they were back in America and the thrill was over, they parted ways, Mik to her full-time job and her ex to the other side of the country. "I worked for them until recently. When I heard my grandmother needed help, I decided to quit that job and come home for a while."

"Quit, huh? Your grandmother told people you were only taking a leave of absence."

She did? Mik didn't know why, other than Abby may have misinterpreted the truth. "No, I quit. It was too stressful. They made us work in teams, competing against each other to get marketing gigs. If our team 'won,' we got bonuses and better networking relationships with the clients who liked our work. You have to understand, they were only paying us minimum wage, so those bonuses made up a bulk of our income." It would have been another story if Mik made around $15 an hour, which could have helped her comfortably pay for her one-bedroom apartment on the eastside without panicking about work. *That wasn't the point, was it? My company wanted us "incentivized."* The execs made money no matter what.

"Sounds rough. I barely make minimum wage out here, but I guess it goes farther."

"Yeah... so, you're an EMT, huh?"

Ariana turned around, one eyebrow raised. "So you've noticed?"

Mik blushed. "I mean, it's kind of unexpected."

"I like helping people. It was something I sort of fell into after realizing that."

"Clearly, you're good at it."

"Am I?"

Well, you put aside our differences to help me. "Yes. Also, you're a Stephen King fan now, so that's another way you've changed."

"Yes. I've changed." That was all Ari said as she rounded a bend in the trail. Mik followed her, of course, but it felt like she was entering some weird gravitational pull that could easily be the end of her.

They were silent for several more minutes as they continued up the trail. Nobody else passed them, either on their way up or coming back down from the summit. *Guess it's not a big day for taking on Wolf's Hill.* Ariana wasn't bothered with physical exertion, since she kept her hands in her pockets and looked as if she were on a leisurely stroll as opposed to a mild hike. Mik wasn't terribly out of shape, but she'd be lying if she said she was totally unbothered by forty-five minute's worth of steady climbing. *Just don't start breathing out of your mouth, and you won't look like a city-slickin' fool!*

The summit was as clear as the rest of the trail had been. Ariana kept her hands in her pocket as she perched atop a smoothed boulder overlooking the valley that dipped down from the west side of the Coast Range. Beyond another small set of hills was the Pacific Ocean, and they said on a good, clear day one could see the surf. Well, Mik had never seen it, even on clear summer days. If somebody wanted to see the ocean from that far away, they got in a car and drove for half an hour. Wolf's Hill simply wasn't tall enough to see that far.

Yet it was tall enough to make Mik glad to sit down.

"So..." Here she went. The moment Mikaiya had been dreading since she realized she was moving back, let alone the day she first saw the new Ariana Mura. "I really, really want to explain what happened that one night."

Ariana snorted. "That *one* night? You mean the one when..."

"Yes. That one." The only reason Mik cut her off was because she couldn't bear to hear the details she already knew. "There's stuff that happened I've never told anyone but my grandma. It's why I had to leave so suddenly."

Mik looked up to find Ari giving her the biggest side-eye of their lives. *Yup. This is when I die.* All alone at the top of an isolated hill. A long, long way down if she "fell" off the wrong side of Wolf's Hill. Ari might still be pissed enough that she booted her ex without thinking. A crime of passion! It would be a fitting end to Mik's strange life.

"Don't see why we need to hash it out," Ariana said. "Not like it happened a year ago."

"No, but I think about it all the time. I'm sure you do, too."

That got a serious furrow of the brows out of Ariana, who was looking more and more likely to bash in Mikaiya's skull. Didn't matter that Ari sat with a cool demeanor and kept her hands to herself. Mikaiya knew what was likely to come should they go down this road. *Yet who am I to stop it? She deserves to know.* They were old enough to understand what had happened.

"I knew you were gonna be in trouble as soon as I saw you were back in town."

"Hey, if you *really* don't want to know what happened, so be it. I won't force you to listen to me."

Ari shook her head. "You wanna know what it looked like *from my end?*" She didn't wait for Mik to respond. "I was some stupid fool waiting for you on the edge of town. I snuck out of my house with a backpack full of crap and waited and *waited,* Mik. I thought something horrible had happened to you. When I finally snuck back home and called your place, your grandma told me that you had already gone to Portland and weren't planning on coming back. Thought she was lying. Maybe she figured out what we planned and put some stop to it on your end." An irritated scoff burst from Ariana's muscular form. "But nope. I found out pretty quick that you really were gone. No word. No nothing." She paused. "It really fucked me up."

Mikaiya couldn't bring herself to look in Ari's direction. Instead, she gazed at the rainy fog rolling through the valley below them. "I'm sorry," she finally said. "I never wanted to hurt you."

"Guess it doesn't matter now. It was a stupid thing, anyway. We should feel so lucky that we didn't get married on a childish whim. What was I going to do? Go with you to Portland? Where you would have this life at college and I would, what? Work at McDonald's to help pay our rent? We would've been miserable."

"Yeah, maybe." Mik had often thought of that, too. How they probably would've lasted for more than one or two years had they gone through with their plans. Except was that the way to find out? At least they wouldn't have yet been burdened by a divorce in Oregon. Mikaiya couldn't remember if the marriage would've been legal in Nevada. It didn't matter, though. To two excited teenagers in love, it was the epitome of their grand romance. And it hurt Ariana as much as being left at the fake altar would have hurt any girl. "I still owe you an apology, though, and an explanation."

Ari looked as if there weren't any good explanations left in that world.

"It was my uncle." Mikaiya exhaled the breath she had kept pent up in her diaphragm, as if she were a singer about to unleash the saddest ballad ever composed. "You remember my Uncle Jake? The guy I told you could never catch us fooling around on the farm?"

Ariana slowly nodded. "Yeah, kinda hard to forget a warning like that."

"He hated lesbians. His mom – um, I mean, my grandma – is one, you know? He blamed her for ruining the family. When my grandma left her husband 'cause she didn't wanna live the lie no more, she took her kids with her, and they never heard from my grandpa again." From all accounts, there wasn't much missing from their lives. "My uncle took it really hard. Blamed her for it all, you know? Even when he got control of the old farm, his dad was no longer around. Held in all that bitterness. My mom wasn't a lesbian, so his ire kinda skipped over her. 'Cept once he found out I was probably 'that way' too, he warned me." That was putting it lightly. "Anyway, both my grandma and he found out about our plans because I was stupid and left my map of our road trip from here to Vegas on my bed. My grandma laughed it off and told me to go ahead, do it. Wasn't like it was anything but symbolic back then. But my Uncle Jake told me that if we ran off, I might as well not come home, because he'd kill us both."

Ariana was silent as she processed it. Or, at least, Mik assumed that's what she was doing. *You're so hard to read now. Did I do that to you?*

"You believed him, huh?"

"He scared the pants off me, that's for sure." Mik sighed again. Rain continued to drizzle on top of her head and down the back of her jacket.

Dust turned to mud around her feet. That old and tired scent of precipitation was at full force now. Even in Portland, it had been a familiar scent. One that both lulled Mik into a false sense of security and sent her clawing at the walls closing in around her. *It was one of the first things I smelled after that time I kissed you, Ari.* It was also the scent that greeted her that first night in Portland, when she had run away from fears that may have never come to fruition. "I packed up most of my things that night and ran away. I thought that if I put that distance between us, my uncle wouldn't hurt you." He couldn't hurt anyone now. Uncle Jake was six feet under after all his bitterness gave him a heart attack. Abby Marcott had lost both of her children. No wonder she didn't mind having Mikaiya around again.

Ari stood up from the boulder, her feet carrying her to the fenced edge of the summit. Two birds flew past her face. The rain came a little harder now, but nobody was as unperturbed by it as Ariana. "You didn't think to tell me before you high-tailed it out of town?"

"My only thoughts were of getting the hell out before he hurt either of us." Mik scratched her scalp beneath her hat. "I was a kid. *We* were kids. I didn't realize what the consequences would be leaving you behind like that. Now I know."

"Do you?"

Mikaiya looked up from her lap, which had become damp from the moisture filling the air. Through a foggy, dreary haze she saw Ariana standing near the fence, her strong body liable to crack Mik's head open. *That ain't why you got big and tough, though, huh?* Ariana buffed up to protect herself and to save others. That much was clear. Then again, how much of it was natural, anyway? Maybe Ari was always destined to stack up a bit when she matured. Hitting the gym and having a physically demanding job only aided that inevitable.

"Do I what?" Mik asked.

"Do you really know what the consequences were?"

Bristling, Mikaiya looked away again. "I guess not."

"You didn't only fuck me up, Mik. The whole town treated it as the scandal of the summer, because obviously people found out. Gossip said that I asked you to run away with me and you freaked out and booked it to the city. Depending on who you ask, I was either the wilting flower petal plucked too soon and left in the rain, or I was the thorny bitch who drove one of Paradise Valley's best and brightest out of town."

Mik groaned. "I'm so sorry. That was never my intention."

"You know the saying. Intentions ain't magical. Doesn't matter what you intended, Mik. All that matters is what happened."

Good gracious, wasn't this one of the reasons Mik dreaded coming back home? Seeing what her actions had wrought?

"You can excuse what happened that night as you being a young idiot." Ariana turned back toward her. Rain covered her face. She remained as unperturbed as the birds in the trees. "You can't excuse the past few years. You ran and hid. You stayed hiding. You never once called me, wrote me a letter, nothing. I've spent the past ten years trying to figure out what the hell I did to make you take off as if we hadn't spent two years together. I know everything feels the worst when you're young, dumb, and in love, but I'm almost thirty years old and still feel sick to my stomach when I think about that night."

Mikaiya forced herself to meet Ari's fierce gaze. "I'm sorry. It was wrong to abandon you like that. It was worse to act like nothing had happened for so long."

A soft snort blew out of Ari's nose. "Well, you're here now. Let's move on."

Something about the way she said that filled Mik with more shame. *God protect the kid who has her for a mother. She knows exactly how to sound so whatever while making you feel like the biggest pile of shit in the room.* Maybe that only applied if a woman had a reason to feel like a giant pile of crap. "I only wanted you to know what happened. I didn't leave that night for no good reason. I... I still loved you, okay?"

Ari went from "moving on" to a frozen statue in two seconds. Her paling face was exacerbated by the dark coloring of her clothes. *Jesus, I am so sorry.* Mikaiya would never be able to make it up to her ex. The damage had been too great. She should have known that it wasn't only their breakup that would damage Ariana. The gossip would have been ripe... for *months.* What was more salacious than one of the most well-known lesbian couples from Clark High School having a sudden, mysterious breakup? Everyone knew that Mikaiya had been accepted to college. There were questions about what would happen to her relationship, but none of it was serious. The worst that would happen was a mutual breakup either right before she went off to school or after their romance fizzled out due to separation. Some may have assumed Ari would move to Portland with Mik. *I don't remember what we planned now.* A sham marriage to make themselves feel good. Mikaiya had wanted to call this woman her wife. This woman whom she hardly recognized anymore.

No. She recognized her.

Her nose was the same. The way her brows furrowed whenever someone said something distasteful was a grand reminder of high school class discussions. Her voice was a little deeper, but Ariana still spoke like she was about to launch into a conversation about her latest fascination in the media. The longer Mik looked at her, the more nostalgic she became... and the more her heart hurt.

Mikaiya stood up. "I'm really sorry, Ari." She could apologize a hundred times, and it still wouldn't break down the wall between them. "I did it because I thought it would protect us. I should have said something, though. I should have come back as soon as I heard my uncle was dead. By then I was a senior in college, and..." No, she had to stop with the excuses. Those were feeble reasons she fed herself when she lived in the moment. "*I can't go back now. It's too late. She wouldn't want to see me. I've moved on. I have a new girlfriend now.*" Girls came and went. There was a reason none of them stayed around for long.

None of them made me feel as much love as Ari did.

Mik had brushed it off as young love. That kind of love that felt so real, so triumphantly yet so stupidly pure. The one great love to last the rest of their lives. High school sweethearts that beat all modern odds and stood as a testament to traditional values when it came to love. That's what they thought they had back then. For all Mik knew, Ari was two seconds away from punching her in the face. Or maybe getting her new girlfriend to do it for her.

Did she have a new girlfriend? Had there been others for Ari like there had been for Mik?

Why did she care so much?

Because look at her! I still love her!

Mik gasped. The sudden reaction made Ari take a step forward, probably some EMT instinct she couldn't prevent.

"It's fine if you never forgive me." Mikaiya wanted to amend that with "*I don't deserve your forgiveness,*" but that would make it more about *her* than how she had wronged Ari ten years ago. Ten whole years of doubt and heartbreak. Hell, could Mik ever forgive herself? "I only want to know that we're going to be okay. As acquaintances." She wouldn't hold out hope that they could ever be anything more again.

The rain came harder. Both Mik and Ari were so frozen in the moment, staring into each other's vacuous faces, that they couldn't be bothered to shake off the rain or run for cover. What was the point? This was probably the warmest they had felt together since the night before everything fell apart.

"I don't know," Ariana said. "I don't know how I feel right now. You coming back to town has really dug up a lot of bad feelings I had. Thought I was over it, you know?" She swallowed. "We're grown adults now. We should get over that stuff we did as kids."

That almost felt like a knife right to Mik's heart. "That 'stuff' was being in love for two years, Ari."

"Yeah, well, it's been long over."

She still feels something for me, doesn't she? Mik wasn't sure what she expected when she came back to town. The only Ariana she imagined still having feelings for her was one who looked exactly as she did back in high school. Not this new Ari who looked like she had never been in love before. *I did that to her. I did* this *to her!* Mik swallowed the bile rising in her throat and suddenly noticed the water on her face. She wanted it off. All of it. Down her hands and cast to the ground, which absorbed each drop of rain and created enough mud to slide them both down Wolf's Hill.

"I'm *sorry!*"

It didn't matter how much she said it, though. She could be sorrier than she ever had a right to be, but it didn't change the past. Ari had no reason to forgive her. Damnit, why would she? Her heart hadn't merely been broken. It had been *shattered*. How could Mikaiya have ever done that to the girl she supposedly loved? Even if she thought she was protecting Ariana from the wrath of an unhinged man... she should have offered an explanation. She should have called, written something, or at least had her grandmother explain what happened. Instead? Mik had been the ultimate coward. It had been all about her and her safety. She could rationalize it was about Ariana, too, but in the end, Mik cared more about her own hide. Didn't matter why. Because she knew how mean her uncle could be? Because she was excited to start her new life at college? Because she was anxious to attach herself to the only girl she had ever loved? Where did Mik's romantic nature end and her fear of long-term commitment begin?

Yet she could think that... then realize how so many of her other relationships fizzled because she always compared those women to the one standing before her. Seeing how Ariana turned out only made that worse.

"Fuck you, Mik."

She deserved that. The caustic words that only a woman so scorned could utter.

Mikaiya was prepared to turn around and head down the hill by herself. She would leave Ariana here to stew in her thoughts and, with any luck, their future encounters would be pleasant at best. They would avoid each other.

People would continue to gossip about what happened between them, but they would show a boring-enough front to make them back the hell off.

Hopefully.

Still, the pain in Mikaiya's heart was almost too much to bear. *I hurt her. I hurt the only woman who ever mattered to me. I hurt the girl I was gonna marry.* How did they both move on from this? How did Mik make peace with what she did, and how did Ari put this behind her and meet someone new? Someone who would treat her with more respect than Mik had?

Could Mikaiya walk away?

She didn't know which one of them hurt more in that moment. She didn't know which one of them was better off leaving the other behind. All Mik knew was that she wanted to throw her arms around Ariana. If she was pushed away, then so be it. At least then she would know where they stood with one another.

"I'm sorry," she whispered one last time, her arms locked around Ari's broad shoulders. Her ex remained frozen in Mik's sudden embrace. "I fucked up a really good thing."

After a few seconds of hesitation, Ari hugged her back.

Chapter 10

ARIANA

This was the kind of moment she dreamed about but never anticipated. The day Mikaiya came back and said she was sorry.

Don't fall for it you idiot... Ariana chanted that in her head as she wrapped her arms around her ex's body, the rain continuing to patter against their heads and down their jackets. *She doesn't really mean it. She's only saying it to save her ass.* For all Ari knew, that story about Jake had been a lie. Who knew how grand Mik's imagination had become? Besides, the Mikaiya she once loved would have still offered some explanation, yeah?

But she hadn't. The Mik she had loved never existed. Either that, or Ariana had been completely blinded by her young feelings to see what kind of girl possessed her heart.

The moment of tenderness they shared on top of Wolf's Hill was Ariana's Achilles heel. She allowed her memories to swallow her whole, bringing her back into that headspace she once occupied as a teenager convinced that she had the whole love and relationship thing figured out. If only their young love hadn't been on display to their whole town. If only that town wasn't so small that everyone and their kids still remembered the Ballad of Ariana Mura and Mikaiya Marcott. Years had passed before the townsfolk stopped looking at Ari with such pity, and this was after she got fit and became an EMT that saved half the lives in town.

Ari couldn't tell if Mik was crying into her shoulder. She didn't care. Any tears they shed would be washed away by the rain caressing their faces. No chance to be embarrassed. Not when Ariana succumbed to one thing she had wanted most over those past ten years.

One damn kiss. Just *one* to give them closure after being torn apart so suddenly.

I still love you. That reality haunted Ariana as she slammed her lips against Mik's, swearing to herself that she could pull away and end this at any time. She only wanted a little closure. Enough to help her sleep at night. She didn't care if Mikaiya could sleep. Only that she was here, kissing Ari back and tasting as sweet as she had back in high school.

Damnit. It was supposed to be a simple kiss. Since when did Ari ever plan on shoving her tongue down Mik's throat and clutching her like she was about to skip town again?

I still love you. I hate how weak that makes me.

Mik didn't still love her. Not even a kiss as hard as the rain now falling on their heads could change that opinion. In the past ten years, Ari had grown in stature and attitude. She learned to stand up straight and carry herself with a confident gait that broadcasted her change in personality. *Have I changed, though? Two weeks in town, and this asshole has her lips on me.* Some things never improved. Ari could mature, but she couldn't keep her hands and mouth off the girl who broke her heart. Deep down, she wanted to believe that their grand romance could happen again.

You fool.

Her self-admonishments only made her kiss Mik harder, as if she deserved to do this to herself. A just punishment for a fool who didn't know what was good for her. Yes, yes, clearly what Ariana needed was *more* of Mik's pain. Ari may be big enough to crush her ex in her arms, but was she big enough to protect their hearts? Didn't she realize that the most dangerous thing she could do was reopen those old wounds? The ones that had scarred. Because wounds that deep never truly healed.

They were only ripped open again and again.

Mikaiya met her anxious desires, feeling that deep pain that rumbled beneath their feet. She naturally shrunk within Ari's arms, as if she were the small and demure lady of this ill-fated pair. She couldn't fool Ari, though. Ariana may have once been the sweet and feminine "stick girl," as many of her classmates had called her, but she hadn't completely lost what made her so vibrantly keen to call some girl her protector. *I protect myself now, but I still want someone who can keep the demons away from our door.* Mikaiya could change her makeup, get a fifty-dollar haircut, and put on a fancy pair of boots, but she had barely changed a day. That was Ari's greatest weakness. Facing the older and more mature version of Mikaiya Marcott, the girl who had seduced Ariana after only one conversation in their high school hallways.

You were the first girl I kissed. The first girl I touched. The first one I let touch me. Ariana bet that sex with Mik would be different now. No more fumbling. Just the kind of sex that two grown woman who wanted each other engaged in, with no fear to simmer between them.

That wasn't going to happen. Not here. Not ever, if Ariana were smart enough. Yet she couldn't bring herself to end the kiss she started. This was it. Their last kiss, the one she had craved for ten years.

It would end on her terms. That's all she knew – and cared about.

"Ari..." That was the first thing out of Mik's mouth when Ariana finally turned her head. The wetness on her lips was all rain, no kiss. The taste of freshly fallen precipitation had never been so strong. Neither had the cool rush of blood covering Ari's tongue, as she bit down so hard on it that she feared she'd choke.

Mikaiya was still in her grasp. Small. Weak. Submissive. Three things Ari never thought of her as when they dated. Mik had always been the outgoing and popular one. She had a whole softball team to fuel her ego, and teachers who adored her witty intellect in class. Ariana always considered herself the luckiest girl in Clark High, because she was dating the lesbian equivalent of the star quarterback. *In my humblest of opinions, anyway.* She may never have been cheerleading material, regardless of how others perceived her, but Ariana Mura had always considered herself the perfect foil to Mik's natural extroversion and ability to charm the pants off any woman, regardless of age.

I guess things have changed. That's all Ari could think as she considered the wispy woman in her grasp.

Yet she still wanted her. That was the dangerous thing.

"I'm gonna go." Ari released Mik from her hold, walking away as if they had merely shaken hands instead of made out like heathens on top of a mountain. "See you around. Give your grandma my regards."

"Hey!" Mik threw her arms up toward the sky in disbelief. The rain let up a little, but not enough to keep her from looking like a drowned rat at the summit of Wolf's Hill. "What the hell, Ari? You gonna screw my mouth then get the hell out?"

Ari waved to her ex-girlfriend from over her shoulder. "Sounds familiar, doesn't it?"

"Oh, you bitch!"

Something about the tone in Mik's voice was sweet music to Ari's ears. Sure, it was a dick move to kiss her then dump her out in the middle of nowhere, but wasn't it a form of poetic justice? Their high school English teachers would have *loved* how much Ari had learned literary theory since her regular Cs in English class. *Stephen King has taught me soooo much.* Following him on social media had inspired her to be a little more caustic in real life as well. If he could call his dog Thing of Evil, then she could think of Mik as Ghost of Past Evils. Now Ari was putting Mik firmly into the past with each step she took down the hill.

Mikaiya did not come after her.

By the time Ari reached her truck, the highway and the parking lot were devoid of life. The only other sign of humanity was Mik's truck, and it was as empty as Ari's heart as she turned on her engine and pulled out of the parking lot. She may have been drenched in rain, but she had never felt so refreshed.

Until she got home, anyway.

She first stepped into the mudroom, where she stripped off her wet jacket, scarf, and gloves. The boots were tossed into the corner. Her socks were likewise soaked, which she hadn't noticed until she tried wiggling her toes in a warm room. Those came off, too. The only things she didn't take off were her jeans and pullover, and that was because she didn't know who else might be home.

Nobody, it turned out. Ari had the whole place to herself. She opted to take a hot shower, where she lightly scrubbed the weirdness of the day off her skin.

It wasn't until she turned around and saw her face in the fogged up mirror hanging in the back of the shower that she realized what had happened.

I kissed her. Those lips in her reflection had done the unthinkable. The fantasized, yet unthinkable. *I wasn't supposed to do that.* Ari wasn't supposed to be weak anymore. She was better than that. She could get through one private encounter with Mik and not *kiss her*.

Why had she done that? Was it really weakness? Or something else?

I still love her…

It didn't matter how many times Ariana thought that. It still felt like the first time, every time. Yet instead of feeling the fluttering of a heart falling in love all over again, she only experienced that adrenaline pumping through her veins, warning her that everything was about to come crashing down on top of her head.

She had done the unthinkable. Something she always swore she would never do should Mikaiya come storming back into her life. For every fantasy young Ariana Mura entertained about hugging and kissing Mikaiya again, there were ten more about slapping her and telling her to fuck off forever.

If only Ariana had embraced the correct fantasy that day.

She tapped her forehead against the shower wall, steam evaporating her tears and hot water washing away her pride.

Chapter 11

MIKAIYA

"I'm off again!" Skylar pumped her purse into the air before opening the front door. "Wish me luck for this one! I *really* need a job around here!" She was gone before anyone could wish her well.

Mik crossed her arms on the kitchen table and lowered her head between them. A sigh pushed through the Formica. Although the sun was shining outside for the first time in days, she couldn't bring herself to drink in the rays of much-needed Vitamin D. Took too much effort. Like it took too much effort to check in on her grandmother, who was last seen watching daytime soap operas while furiously working on a knitting project.

It had been two days since Mikaiya went with Ariana up Wolf's Hill and allowed herself to be sucked into the past. *She kissed me. She seriously kissed me, yes?* While Mikaiya didn't doubt the validity of the *kiss,* she refused to believe that it was Ariana who started it. Yet she had, hadn't she? Mik hadn't dreamed it up, had she? Because she would rather die than believe in a world where the woman she still loved so much *hadn't* kissed her first.

Mik was stuck between two impossible worlds. In one, she begged to get the hell away from this place. To forget anything had happened between her and Ari, the girl she tried to forget, although her heart refused. In the other? She pined after Ariana Mura to the point she was willing to lay her heart bare before her, in the hopes that Ari could see how sorry she was. If Mikaiya had the power to change the past, she would have! She knew that now. She knew the reason she was terrified to come back to Paradise Valley wasn't only because she feared facing Ariana again, but also because she feared renewing that love that had never let her go.

The kiss replayed itself in an indefinite loop. Every time something wet or cold touched Mikaiya's lips, she remembered how Ariana had all but shoved her down into the mud, not to beat her up like she deserved, but to cover her in the crazy kind of kisses they used to indulge when they were a crazier pair of kids.

Mikaiya pulled herself away from the table before she suffocated on Formica. She stood in front of the window for an ungodly amount of time, wondering what the hell she should do. What *could* she do? Besides try to get over Ari again? *She doesn't want me. She made that clear*. There may still be something between them, but Mik had ruined it by being the biggest coward Paradise Valley had ever seen. Her reputation would always precede her in that town. She was better off hiding in her grandmother's house until it was time to move on again. Let Skylar get to know everyone by running the errands. Maybe it would help her get a job. God knew Mik needed to start thinking about her future funds. Before this business with Ariana, she had thought about doing freelance marketing consultations. Online, of course. Because she doubted most of the small businesses around Paradise Valley gave a hoot about her big city-girl opinions.

What was a gal to do when she was in this kind of funk? Besides go to her grandmother, of course.

“Want some tea, Grandma?” Mikaiya rummaged through the plastic bin by the toaster. The one full of loose, unmarked tea bags, because who cared about caffeinated vs. decaf, or flavored herbal teas vs. plain black? Oh, well. It was early enough in the day that they could both use a little caffeine. “I’m starting the kettle.”

She heard a gruff affirmative over the latest scandal to besiege the southern Californian community depicted in the current soap opera. Mik remained in the kitchen until the water was boiled and two tea bags in their selected mugs. Mikaiya sniffed the aroma of the bags. Eh.

Peach blossom? Earl gray? She was giving up. *Give me some damn tea.* She wanted the distraction from the shit-show playing in her mind. Besides, a chat with her grandmother might be what she needed. Not what she *wanted,* if her instincts about what they might talk about were correct, but what she needed? Definitely.

With a sigh, she carried out both steaming hot mugs to the living room and found Abby slowly making progress on her scarf. Her glazed-over eyes barely registered what was playing on TV. Jeez… somebody *did* need some caffeine, huh?

"Here you go." Mik placed the mugs on a tray before wheeling it over to her grandmother's seat. "Thought you could use some." She flopped down on the nearby couch, blanket spilling over her. A quick glance toward the front windows told her that no busy-bodies passing by could see her from that far away. *Let's hope it stays that way.* Mik wasn't in the mood for the neighbors to make fun of how she drank her tea while her hair badly needed a combing and her clothes looked like she hadn't changed them in over a day. (She hadn't.) "Anything good on TV?"

Abby grunted again. She didn't touch her tea. Her knitting needles slowed until Mikaiya looked over and saw her grandmother nodding off to sleep. She had been sleeping more and more that week. Doctor said it was normal for a woman recovering from a stroke. Still, why did it make her granddaughter so uncomfortable?

I hate seeing how much older she's getting. Abby had always been that tough rock in Mik's life. She had survived a failed marriage... and the premature death of both children. She had raised a granddaughter when Mik's mother was working herself to death to provide for her daughter's college fund. *At least I made good use of it.* Abby wasn't afraid to get her hands dirty or take care of her own house. Landscaping, renovations... there wasn't anything she couldn't teach herself to do. Even when it was cheaper to hire someone else to do it, Abby Marcott preferred to make it herself. So to see her suffering, let alone showing her age, only served to remind Mikaiya that life was in constant flux.

People came and went. They were born. They died, sometimes unexpectedly. *It's not fair.* Why did most children have to experience this the hard way? Over and over?

"Know who I've been bumping into around town?" Mik blew the steam off her tea and settled into the comfiest crevice of the couch. *I've had many bouts of the flu on this couch. How old is it, anyway? She's had it since I was in what... middle school?* The TV was the newest thing in the room. "Ariana. I knew I was going to bump into her here, but we actually had a talk yesterday. I didn't tell anyone I was going out because I didn't want you to worry about me... Anyway, I told her about why I left graduation night. I'm not sure she believed me. It doesn't matter. She's still pissed. I opened those old wounds. Including for myself." Mik sighed, placing her mug on the end table next to the couch. "I'm sorry. I shouldn't be dragging this up right now. Just making things terribly uncomfortable for everyone." She pushed herself up and turned her head toward Abby. "Grandma?"

No response.

"Grandma?" Mikaiya tossed the blanket to the side and swung her legs back toward the carpet. "You okay?"

The needles were in Abby's lap, and her head against the back of the chair. Her mouth was slightly open… and so were her eyes, which continued to stare at the ceiling as if she couldn't move her neck if she tried.

"Grandma!"

Mikaiya had heard tales about the poor person who found Abby Marcott after her first stroke a few months ago. Mrs. Getty, one of the neighbors down Colorado Street, had stopped by to return a toolset she had borrowed two days before. The lights had been on in the kitchen, but no response had unsettled her until she peered through a side window and saw Abby crouched toward the floor, her body splayed in a most unnatural position. This explanation had, of course, come straight from Mrs. Getty's mouth when she stopped by a week ago to welcome Mikaiya back to Paradise Valley. The way Abby told it, she had called 911 all by herself.

911. That seemed *fairly pertinent* right now.

There were other things Mik could have done. She had seen plenty of "Think FAST" brochures around the house since moving back. Yet none of them applied to the panic rising in Mik's chest as she attempted to get her grandmother to respond to her. All she could think about was calling for someone to come help. Skylar wasn't around. Mrs. Getty probably wouldn't drop by at the perfect time. It was up to Mik, the girl who came home to make sure her grandmother got the care she needed.

When the 911 operator asked about her emergency, Mik barely got the words, "*I think my grandmother is having a stroke,*" out of her mouth. A part of her didn't want it to be true. Another part of her knew it was highly likely that Abby would be sick again before a year had passed since the first stroke. She had done everything she could to get her grandmother enjoying a healthier lifestyle, but diet and taking it easy could only do so much, the doctor said. "*Some people are simply susceptible.*"

An ambulance was dispatched to the house. The ETA was five minutes, during which time Mik was asked to relay information about her grandmother's condition. It was probably more of a tactic to keep Mikaiya calm and focused on something besides her grandmother's ailment, otherwise, what good was she?

Someone pounded on the door.

Mik still wasn't thinking. With the phone plastered to her head, all she could imagine was that someone had picked the *wrong* time to come by for a visit. Instead of seeing one of Abby's old friends on the other side of the door, however, she saw one of the last people she probably needed in her life right now.

"What's going on?" It was Ari, dressed for work and carrying her cases and whatever medical devices she deemed necessary for this call. *Oh my God. How could I forget she was an EMT!* Mik was so trapped in the moment that she had no idea how to prepare for the oncoming guests she was sure to recognize.

"Something about a stroke? Is it your grandmother?"

She didn't wait for an answer. She pushed by Mikaiya, who confirmed with the 911 operator that the ambulance had arrived. A man followed Ariana into the house. They both beelined for Abby, mini flashlights turning on and soft voices filtering through the air.

"Hey, Abby." Ariana knelt beside the chair while the young man unpacked something from a bag. Mik was trapped on the other side of the room, afraid to move, and more afraid to put her phone away. She held it close to her chest and bit the cuticle off her right index finger. She should call or text Skylar. She should go outside for some air. Yet she could do neither, because she was too transfixed on the strange scene unfolding before her.

The part of her that fretted for her grandmother warred with the part that wanted to scream at Ariana to do something, anything.

Anything.

"When did you first notice she wasn't well?" the male EMT asked.

Mik snapped herself back to reality. The one where her grandmother was possibly having another stroke... and the one where her ex came storming back into her life two days after kissing and dumping her on top of Wolf's Hill. Ari was coolly confidant as she moved in that uniform that showcased how at ease she was at her job. Good! Wasn't that what Mik wanted? Capable EMTs who were strong enough to pick people up yet calm enough to get through to them?

"Ms. Marcott?" the man asked again.

"Oh, uh... about ten minutes ago." Mik stepped forward, careful to keep Ariana at a certain distance. "I brought her some tea. Last I had seen her she was knitting and watching TV. Don't know when this started. I had been in the other room most of the morning..."

"Abby? Can you hear me?" Ariana waved one finger before Abby's face. The man checked Abby's vitals while Ariana continued to speak. "Do you know what day it is?"

Whatever sound came out of Abby's mouth, it wasn't English. It probably wasn't a real word in any language. That only made Mikaiya more worried.

"Can you smile for me, Abby?" Two seconds later, Ari turned to her partner and muttered, "She's not responding to my requests. We need to get her to the hospital."

Those words hit Mik right in the chest. "Is she going to be okay?" she asked the EMTs. She didn't care which one answered her.

"I don't know right now." Ari passed her to grab the stretcher on the other side of the front door. "Our main concern is getting her safely to the hospital. Is your friend around here somewhere?"

She must have meant Skylar. "No. She's out." Mik turned on her phone, but the first anxious sob took hold of her. "Why?"

"Wasn't sure if you wanted to ride in the back or not. We'll be taking her to the county hospital." A tiny smirk appeared on her face. "Same one you were at last week."

Two visits in two weeks! What was up with the Marcott house, anyway? "Oh, my God. Is she having another stroke?"

"Possibly. It looks like it." Ari had to tear herself away from her ex to help Abby onto the stretcher. Mik stayed back, tears welling in her eyes. It was all she could do to keep from wailing like a child while she watched the old love of her life and a total stranger load her grandmother onto a stretcher and share their coded words to ensure Abby got into the back of the ambulance with no issue. "Grab her wallet!" Ari called to Mik once they were outside.

Right. There were things Mik could do to help. Things like grabbing her grandmother's satchel with her wallet in it and locking up the house on her way out the door. She had to race back inside when she realized she never turned down the heater. Mik left their undrunk tea in the living room, an unfortunate reminder that things had not gone to plan.

"Let's go!" Ari called across the lawn. More than a few of the neighbors had once again gathered to witness the spectacle erupting. Mikaiya paid them no mind as she raced to the ambulance backed up in the driveway and came within a breath's reach of her ex.

There was no time to say anything. Besides, whatever they wanted to say to one another didn't matter as much as getting Abby to the hospital before she got worse.

"Come on." Ariana took Mikaiya by the hand and helped her into the back of the ambulance, where Abby was secured on her stretcher and awaiting transport. The vehicle hummed to life the moment Ari shut the door and sat next to Abby. Mik was relegated to the other side, where she held her grandmother's satchel in her lap and stared into the pale face of the woman who used to regularly kick the world's ass.

"Tell me she's going to be okay." Mikaiya braced herself as the ambulance turned onto Colorado Street. "Even if you're lying to me, Ari, tell me she's going to be okay."

Ariana looked between Abby and Mik with nothing but pity in her eyes. *I don't want your pity, Ari! I don't want your mind games, don't want your kisses, and sure as hell don't want your stinkin' pity right now!* She wanted reassurance. That her grandmother would live and be better than ever. That *they* were going to be okay. Somehow.

"She's going to be okay, Mik." Ariana said that while looking her ex right in the frightful eyes. "We're doing everything we can to make sure that happens."

Mikaiya doubled over, tears staining her grandmother's satchel. Ariana stayed respectfully silent while focusing her attentions on the patient and making sure they got to the county hospital in record time.

It was the longest twenty-seven miles of Mik's life. Longer than the night she ran away from Paradise Valley and didn't stop until she reached Portland, and the new life that awaited her.

Chapter 12

ARIANA

Ari stood outside Abby Marcott's room, a small bouquet of flowers in her hand. She looked up and down the hallway one more time to ensure that there wasn't anyone else around that intended to visit the invalid in room 203. Fine thing if Ari waltzed in there the moment Mikaiya showed up to check on her grandmother. It was Saturday. Who knew how many people would use one of the biggest days off of the week to come check up on their favorite Ms. Fix-It?

Do it, you big coward. Ariana straightened out her pullover and made sure she had no new stains on her jeans before helping herself into 203. Abby wasn't big enough news to have her own room. She shared this one with a young woman who had her arm up in a cast. Ari bowed her head in acknowledgment as she continued toward the window, where Abby sat up in her bed and futzed with the TV remote.

"Afternoon, Abby." Ari startled the woman when she said hello from the other side of the curtain. Then again, it wasn't heart attacks that people worried about with Ms. Marcott. It was more strokes, like the one Thursday afternoon. One could hardly tell now, however. Abby may have had a face that screamed she couldn't smile if she wanted, but that was usual for her. "Came by to say hi and see how you're doing."

"Ari, dear." Abby settled back into her bed. Only one side of her mouth was functioning properly, but she didn't let that stop her from attempting to be a gracious hostess in her little corner of the hospital. "So nice of you to come by. I understand you're the one that came to my house again? We really must stop catching up with these circumstances hanging over us."

That got a snort out of Ari, who looked for a decent place to set her small vase of flowers. She had picked them up from the Paradise Flowers booth at the farmer's market. Ari didn't know much about the pretty florist who worked there, but when she said she was visiting an old friend in the hospital, she was given the most price-conscious yet soothing bouquet she had ever seen. *Good to know*. Ariana didn't have a lot of money, but she liked giving it to local businesses.

"You know who you're getting when you call 911." Ari sat in the creaking chair next to Abby's bed. "Unfortunately for your granddaughter."

Abby attempted to chuckle. Or, at least, Ari assumed that's what that pathetic sound was. *I lied to Mik when I said her grandmother would be okay*. Ariana had no idea of knowing what would happen to Abby Marcott. Her job was to assess situations, apply applicable treatments that were within her power, and transport patients to the hospital when necessary. So, that's what she had done. *I knew it was bad, though*. The first time she encountered Abby in her home that year, it was to respond to that initial, fateful call. Abby had been lucid enough to respond to some questions, at least, even if she didn't do so with the greatest of grace. Yet Ariana couldn't say if this last call had been due to a stroke. Between doing her job in an emergency situation *and* dealing with her panicking ex, she could barely focus on one thing at a time.

"I'm grateful that Mik is back in town." Ari barely understood the words coming out of one side of Abby's mouth, but she definitely picked up on the sentiment. "How about you?"

Something cinched in the pit of Ari's stomach. "What do you mean?"

"I was still somewhat lucid before I blacked out," Abby continued. "I heard her say something about meeting with you to talk. Is that true?"

Ariana shifted in her seat. "Yeah. She wanted to explain a few things, I guess."

"Did she tell you about my son?"

"If you mean Uncle Jake... yeah. I didn't know if it was true or not, though." Sheesh. This was not what Ariana had in mind when she came to visit the woman she considered a second grandmother back in the day. *You always fed me whenever I came to visit.* The Mura family struggled with poverty in underemployed Roundabout, but Ariana never went hungry as a child, even before someone like Abby stepped up to send her home with Tupperware full of stews and leftover mashed potatoes. Yet it had been nice to get a good meal three to four times a week and take the pressure off her own mother.

Those were the memories she would rather rehash, if Abby insisted on rehashing *anything.* Not what might have happened between her and Mik that week, let alone ten years ago. *Don't we have enough memories together, Abby?* Here was hoping it was her aging, ailing brain that made her drag up the shit instead of focusing on more pleasant things.

"It was true," Abby candidly said.

Ariana swallowed something sour.

"My son was a little jackass," Abby continued, although she sounded more than winded, perhaps pained, to drag up these memories. Ari was simply impressed that the woman could remember these things right now. Maybe she would recover, after all – assuming she followed the doctor's orders to keep taking it easy and to eat more than red meat every day.

"Always had been, but when I left his father and moved to Paradise Valley, he took it really hard. Blamed me for things beyond anyone's control. Kids are like that, though." She slowly rolled her head over to the other side of her pillow. It was now easier to see the sag on the left side of her face. "They need someone to blame when their lives are hard. Guess adults aren't so different, either."

"Yeah. Guess not." Ariana sure loved having someone to blame for all the heartache she suffered years ago. And a little bit today. Sure seemed to happen to a lot of people she knew.

"Still, all that drama surprised me, too. Didn't think my son had it in him to threaten his own kin like that. But there was a reason he liked working out of town for most of his life. Didn't like people. Didn't like it when they didn't follow his rules, you know. Never said anything to me because I was his mom. Never said anything to his sister because she followed the rules, outside of never marrying Mik's dad. I guess he wanted something better for Mikaiya. Whatever that meant to him."

Ariana didn't know what to say.

"You have to forgive Mik. She did what she thought was right. Don't get me wrong." Abby attempted to chuckle. "I wanted to beat her ass when I found out she left to go to Portland. I won't lie. I was a little relieved she didn't run off with you."

That made Ari's ears perk up.

"You two were a nice couple, but I don't know how you would've handled the city. I always figured you would have to break up. Girded myself for that inevitable thing. Merely didn't think it would happen that night. Let alone that way. Ah... well."

"I wish someone would have told me."

"I thought you knew for the longest time. When I realized you had no idea a few years ago, I thought about telling you. Then I decided it was best to not drag it up. Mik was determined to stay away from this town. I figured there must be a good reason. So… I never said anything. Not even when she said she was moving back in with me."

Ariana didn't know how to process this information. She would never stop being upset that *somebody* didn't tell her the truth behind graduation night. If not Mik, then shouldn't Abby have said something? Ari couldn't get over being abandoned in the dark of night, scared that something terrible had happened until the dawning realization that Mik had left her behind finally claimed her. *It was the shock that nearly killed me.* Ari knew a lot of about shock as an EMT. It either made people feel more capable than they actually were, or it crippled them to such depths of despair that there was almost no pulling them out and convincing them to save their own stupid lives. She usually saw the former more than the latter. Car crash victims walking away, only to collapse half-dead once they realized half their ribs were broken, were the most likely candidates. But it happened to people who had witnessed terrible things. People who had terrible things happen to them. Ari knew both fairly well by that point in her life.

Had Mik been in shock as well? Did she save their hides, but forget to say anything because she couldn't yet recover from how much her uncle hurt her?

Maybe she hadn't been a coward, after all. Maybe she simply did what was best for them. She had been a kid, after all. She said so herself.

"I've been angry at her for a really long time," Ari said, unsure if Abby heard her. "Didn't realize how angry I still am until she came back to town."

"Anger has a way of festering inside of you until you can no longer contain it," Abby weakly said. "I saw it happen with my son. Maybe you're not a risk to other people, but take care that it doesn't rule your life and relationships with others."

The color was slowly draining from Abby's face. Ari stood up and said her farewells, content with their short conversation if it meant giving the elderly woman some much-needed rest. God knew how much she had expended herself speaking to a woman who had harbored enough resentment to power the machines monitoring her vitals.

Maybe she really did care for me. Ariana was in a fog as she left the hospital and climbed into her truck way out in the visitors' parking lot. *Maybe she really did do what she thought was best for us.* She sat behind the wheel of her truck, watching the rain slowly drip down her windshield. The soothing sounds almost lulled her into a doze, until the chill cut through her pullover and she was compelled to finally start the engine.

Maybe she still has feelings for me. Mikaiya could be a lot of things – brash, self-centered, an occasional idiot – but she had never been callous or cruel until that night. Those two years of being the happiest couple in Clark High weren't merely a lesson in love's cruel intentions. They weren't only a warning of how badly things could go when a girl gave over too much of her heart too soon. They were a stepping stone to becoming the adults that *both* Mikaiya and Ariana saw in their mirrors today.

One man had wanted to ruin them, for no other reason than bitterness about things beyond his control. Well, he had succeeded. For a few years, at least.

Ariana drove back into town with a million things on her mind. The least of which were what she wanted to have for dinner on her day off, or if it was worth watching one of her usual shows that night. She was more absorbed in the past, and how it reflected upon her today. Every time she glanced at her reflection in the rearview mirror, she wondered if she would see the same thing had Mik never skipped town ten years ago.

If, instead, they had driven to Vegas and been married by a man in an Elvis costume.

"Jesus, we were dumb." Ariana laughed as she entered Paradise Valley's city limits. "Woo. Imagine being *that* dumb again."

She'd have her chance soon enough.

Chapter 13

MIKAIYA

"When are you going to make your *grand* apology, though?" Skylar wedged her thumb into Mik's side. Their stroll through the farmer's market that fine Sunday was supposed to be exercise, since it was the first non-rainy day in almost a week. *The rain hasn't stopped since Ariana kissed me on top of Wolf's Hill.* Every time Mik thought about it, she caught herself staring into the cloudy distance. A chill tickled her arms beneath her flannel every time the breeze kicked up. She could hardly feel it, however. She was too warmed by the fluttering of butterflies in her body. How could it be helped? *I'm in love.* A hopeless love. A renewed love. A hopelessly renewed love that should have made her excited to be alive… yet all it did was make her nostalgic.

Skylar tapped her on the shoulder.

"Did you hear me, Mik? You need to kick your butt into gear and properly apology to that ex of yours. Ain't no way you're either moving on or moving *up* from her unless you get down on your knees and beg her to forgive you. At least!"

"What are you talking about? On my *knees*?" Yeah, that did a great job getting Mik's attention. The thought of getting down on one or two knees in front of Ariana conjured a very different scenario. *Didn't I do that when I asked her to run off to Vegas with me?* Yikes. "What's this about a grand apology?"

"Like in romance novels, duh. Don't you know anything?" When Mikaiya was compelled to shake her head, Skylar let out a mighty sigh and continued. "You have to find some grand gesture to prove your love to her! Then she can make her final decision about whether she still wants you or not!" She cocked her head when she realized Mik still wasn't giving her the answer she sought. "You… do still love her, right?"

Mikaiya cocked her eyebrow, hoping that the young family checking out hand carved toys in a nearby stall couldn't see them. "You barely know about this, Sky. Since when are you an expert on my old relationships with the locals?"

"I've been *all over this stupid town.*" How did that come out in a controlled growl instead of an outburst that shook the townsfolk to their sensitive cores? "Applying to jobs, getting to know the unspoken rules… do you know how many times I've had to hear your sob story from everyone in town? Jesus, you have no idea. I've heard so many versions of the romance between you and this Ariana Grande or whatever that I…"

Mik was laughing too much for Skylar to continue.

"What?"

"Ariana *Grande?* Oh, wow." Mikaiya clutched her hand to her stomach. "That's rich.

Whew. The thought of her being anything like the singer…"

"Very funny. Sorry if that's the only person I associate the name *Ariana* with."

"I wonder how many times people have given her crap for that?"

Skylar crossed her arms and leaned back, a sly grin dotting her face. "You've still got it bad for her, don't you? Knew it. My favorite version of the story was the one where Ariana climbed the hill and watched for your return. Dunno how that was supposed to work, but who cares? It's straight out of some tragic love story! Hey!" She slapped her hand against Mik's arm. "Bet she still loves you, too!"

"What makes you say that? *Any* of that?" How dare she put those thoughts in Mik's head? Honestly!

"Because you're blushing like the most lovesick puppy in this town. Trust me. I've seen more lovesick lesbians these past two weeks than I ever did back in Portland."

"Don't let the locals hear you say that. You'll never shake the 'tourist' label."

"Now, now, don't turn it back on me! We've got to figure out a way for you to make your grand gesture!"

"I'm still not sure what that means."

One dramatic eyeroll later, Skylar hauled Mik back through the city hall parking lot, where the monthly farmer's market took place. They were surrounded by greens, buds, and handmade soaps and gifts, but nothing Skylar looked at screamed *Ariana.* Soap was passé as a gift now. Besides, it might say she smelled bad. Not exactly the message Mik wanted to convey to the ex she desired to make amends with... if not more.

"Flowers!" Skylar pointed to the booth nearest the road. There, swimming in a small garden of buds that could withstand the cooler temperatures – or at least for two or three hours – was the local florist carefully tending to petals and stems. She hardly had a care for the two women racing up to her stall as if they needed flowers *right now,* or else their lives would come to a terrible end. "Get her some flowers, Mik! Which ones are her favorite?"

Mikaiya finally shook her friend off her. "I don't know!" She also didn't know how flowers were supposed to solve her romantic conundrum. *Flowers? For Ari?* In what universe would a woman like *her* want flowers, of all things? She'd probably be offended.

Then again… Ariana Mura was once the girl who made daisy chains and wrapped them around her head before following Mik up to her uncle's barn. Who knew? Maybe she still harbored a girlish fondness for some of the world's simplest beauties.

"Can I help you?" A kind face appeared from behind a hanging pot full of bright red flowers. The florist's black hair was capped beneath a lavender-colored beanie, its brim almost covering her eyes. It reminded Mik how chilly it was that day. She hadn't bothered to wear a hat. Her Oregonian pride didn't let her unless it was as low as twenty or raining so hard she couldn't see the town through the showers.

Skylar pushed Mik forward. "My friend here wants to apologize to her ex for the terrible way she dumped her." *Thanks, Sky! That's really helpful!* Mikaiya would have turned around and bopped her friend on the nose if she weren't so humiliated. "You got anything that says, 'I'm really sorry and I'm still madly in love with you?'"

"Hey!" Mikaiya protested. "She doesn't need to know about that."

"There are many flowers that can express that sort of sentiment." The florist's meek voice was almost inaudible over the passing automobile traffic on Main Street. Mik wasn't complaining. She was still planning Skylar's demise. Would anybody notice if she went missing? Ugh. Probably. "As for one particular flower… not so much. I suggest a tasteful bouquet. We could combine yellow roses, which is the international symbol for being sorry," she held up two yellow roses by their fragile stems, "and a few red roses to show your heartfelt feelings. Oh! How about we sprinkle it with some lily of the valley I have over here?"

Mikaiya still wasn't quite sure how she got wrapped up in buying Ariana a bouquet. Yet that was her card swiped through an attachment on the florist's phone, and that was her best friend squealing like she was about to be the maid of honor at the Vegas wedding of the year.

Depending on how Ariana reacted to her gift, Skylar might be.

Chapter 14

ARIANA

"Hazelnut latte, please." Ari slumped against the front counter at Heaven's Café, where the owner was the only one on duty and more than happy to help out the haggard woman stumbling in for some caffeine. "Twelve ounces, I guess."

Heaven cocked one of her slender eyebrows, hand on her hip and the other bracing against the counter where Ari now lay her head. "You sure you don't wanna go for sixteen? Why not a whole pound of latte?"

"Because it's after three," Ariana muttered. "I've got an early shift tomorrow."

Chuckling, Heaven took the debit card protruding from Ari's grasp. "You didn't work today?"

"Nah. Get more Saturdays off." All the better to visit invalids in the hospital. *I didn't visit Mik, though.* To be fair, Ariana already knew how Mik was doing since she was the one to deliver her ex to the hospital. Besides, Mik was in the hospital on days Ariana had to work! Did anyone know how difficult it was to coordinate hospital visits out of town when...

Right. She could've visited Mik while on break *at* the hospital. Not like Ariana didn't spend half her days there sometimes... depending on whether it was hunting or fireworks season...

"One hazelnut latte, coming right up." Heaven turned around and grabbed a cup out of its dispenser. Ariana pulled herself away from the counter, although there was nobody in line behind her. Even on a Saturday, Heaven's was relatively quiet in the middle of the afternoon. The cozy little café was a haven for the local artists and digital nomads who didn't have an office of their own. Heaven often joked that it was the writers, the sketchers, and the independent contractors chained to their laptops who kept the place open. That may be so, but it made it difficult to find a place to sit outside of the big table by the front window. It was usually packed in the morning when friends met up to chat, and families went out to grab a small bite to eat. That day, however... Ari was a sitting duck when she plopped down at the big table adjacent to Main Street.

The day was nice enough to bring out the crowds. So many of the townsfolk looked as if they hadn't seen sunlight in six months. Never mind a single week. Ari couldn't blame them. Just because she was used to being rained on, didn't mean she liked it. Okay, so maybe she liked it. A little. There was something to be said for the cleansing power of nature's tears.

Ha, ha! I'm so funny! 'Cause it was totally cleansing when I kissed my ex in the rain!

The café door opened and closed next to her.

"Hey!" It was Anem Singer, sprung free from her eternal post at the main checkout counter over at the supermarket. Her bushy red hair couldn't obscure the giant smile on her face, but it *could* hide her long-term friends behind her. *Great. A bunch of people I went to high school with.* Ariana spared them a small, friendly smile as half the town descended upon Heaven at the front counter. Anem stayed behind, because she was that kind of socializer.

"How's it going, Ari?" Anem helped herself to the chair across from her old school pal. *We were never really friends...* That was the thing about a small school that served two small towns. You may not be friends with everyone, but you were definitely some kind of acquaintance. The same was true for upperclassmen and underclassmen. A bubbly, friendly gal like Anem? Everyone knew her. Everyone might not have liked her, per se, but they definitely knew her. She *definitely* knew them.

And all their personal business going all the way back to high school.

"Things are fine. Just got back from visiting Abby Marcott at the county hospital."

"Oh! I heard what happened! Is she doing okay?"

"Yeah, she had another stroke. Guess she'll be okay. She was pretty tired, but cognizant enough to make me feel sixteen again." She didn't have to explain any further than that. Anem knew better than most what it meant to feel *sixteen* in Paradise Valley. Had nothing to do with hormones and everything to do with every adult knowing better than them.

"Did you bump into Mik while you were up there?"

"Huh? No." Thank God. "Why?"

"I saw her down at the farmer's market a little while ago. With that new girl." Anem shrugged. "She was buying flowers from Meadow. Assumed they were for her grandma."

"Guess so." Ari must have missed Mik at the hospital, because she didn't see any other flowers in there. While she had assumed Abby would tell her granddaughter who had come to visit, Ari was now treated to the scenario where Mikaiya, weighed down by a bouquet of freshly cut flowers, asked, "*Where did this paltry little thing come from?"* Ariana couldn't help it. EMT pay didn't exactly buy huge bouquets. Not like those marketing salaries did. "How are things at the shop?" It took every bit of restraint within her to refrain from calling the supermarket, "*Ted's Ripoff.*" The owner took every liberty to price gouge the locals in the name of "shipping costs," but everyone knew he only got away with it because of his monopoly. There was talk of a Dollar General opening sometime soon, but the town was of a mixed opinion about how good that would be for the locals. Some competition was desperately needed in Paradise Valley. Yet was a corporate store the answer?

Anem launched into the latest gossip from Ted's Ripoff while her friends dithered over Heaven's menu and decided to spring for a late lunch. Ariana barely paid attention. Kinda hard to when a giant bouquet of yellow and red flowers passed behind her, distracting Anem.

"Whoa, would you look at those?" She was more excited when the deliverywoman popped into Heaven's the moment she saw who sat by the window.

"Hey, Ari!" a deep yet excited voice rumbled through the café, "got some flowers for you! Was running them down to your place, but then I saw you in here!"

Anem's shock was the most palpable thing in the room. More intense than the dread rising in Ariana's throat. "You've gotta be kidding me."

Heads turned when the vase holding a bouquet large enough to overtake the table was set down. The overpowering aroma of roses and whatever those funny little white flowers were blotted out the hazelnut latte Heaven personally brought. She had a whole line of women waiting to get their caffeine and food, yet everyone was so enamored by the buzz of activity in the front corner that nobody thought twice about the only barista on duty getting a front-row view of the goings-on in her café.

"What's this now, Ari?" She put her hands on her hips and clicked her tongue. "Last time I had live flowers in my café, I got complaints from customers with allergies!" Her big, genial smile was the only reason Ariana wasn't profusely apologizing for something she couldn't control. The deliverywoman laughed to explain that Meadow had sent her on this "special errand" from the farmer's market.

"I was taking my break from the Bryer's Wool stall when Meadow asked if I knew where Ariana lives. Said sure! I'm pretty good friends with one of her roommates." Ah, so that was where Ari recognized this woman. Great. Everyone in town was somehow related to her and whatever drama currently cooked her. "Y'all saved me a trip, though. Think I'll get everyone at Bryer's a coffee while I'm here. How about it, Heaven?"

The proprietress shrugged. "You'll have to get in line. Although I'm not sure what's going on right now."

Anem snatched the card out of the bouquet before Ariana could find it. "Hey!" Ari reached across the table to get it back, but Anem had already ripped it open and passed it to one of her friends. The game of keep away that erupted must have delighted the other patrons in Heaven's, because Ari and her giant bouquet had yet to drop their attentions. One of the newcomers to town, a young woman who always wore colorful scarves on her head, approached with a smidge of curiosity in her bright brown eyes.

"It's very beautiful!" She clapped her hands in excitement. It only served to stir up everyone else. "Yellow roses are my favorite! Are those lilies of the valley, too?"

"Don't yellow roses mean you're sorry or something?" someone else asked. "Do red roses mean she wants to sleep with you?"

"Who is it from? You got a secret admirer, Ari?"

Anem ended up with the card again. Ariana conceded defeat, but only because she didn't want to make a huge scene by cussin' everyone out and knocking over this expensive-looking bouquet. *Meadow ain't cheap.* Ari would know. She had bought Abby's get well flowers from the Paradise Flowers' stall earlier that day. Meadow had a knack for creating gorgeous floral designs, and she never let a bad bud get out into the world, but she definitely charged for the service. At least she was always busy in the summer, when every lesbian within a hundred mile radius came to Paradise Valley to get married…

"What's it say, Anem?" Heaven asked.

Ariana braced herself, hands clasped over her mortified face. Yellow roses meant you were sorry? Red roses meant you were in love? Those other white things were lilies? No wonder her sinuses were stuffing. She was allergic to lilies.

Anem cleared her throat before reading a private note out loud to the whole class. "'*I'm sorry. Can we try again?*'" She frowned. There's no name. Darn!

Heaven snorted. So did half the room. The only ones who were disappointed were either too young to remember or had moved in too late to appreciate the Ballad of Ariana Mura and Mikaiya Marcott.

"Oh…" Anem's eyes widened. "*Oh!*"

"Give me that." Ariana snatched the note back. Sure enough, that was Mik's cursive handwriting returning her longing gaze. *I can't believe it.* Couldn't she, though? Mikaiya definitely had a thing for public debacles. She also adored her little love notes. How many had Ari found in her locker back in high school? How many ended up in her backpack, or in her notebooks? That was how they communicated before cell phones became more ubiquitous in Paradise Valley than Blackberries.

The chuckling from her surrounding audience ended abruptly. Ari glanced up from her crumpled note and figured out everyone had been distracted by something on the other side of the window. She was afraid to turn around.

Ah, yes. Being afraid was quite the good idea. Because Ariana immediately regretted turning around in her seat.

Mikaiya stood on the sidewalk, looking back at her in mild shock. The new girl she brought to town was beside her, totally confused until she realized what they were looking at in one of the town's only cafes.

"Oooh," Heaven muttered to the other women around her. "This is gonna be good."

Ariana turned back around with a huff. She was trapped. Couldn't get out of her seat without disrupting the whole café, and couldn't turn her nose up at them because it meant seeing the last person she wanted to acknowledge right now. Didn't help that her stomach was a swarm of mixed feelings. The kiss from earlier that week. The horrifying realization that she had never really gotten over Mikaiya and the love they once shared. And the reminders that what had happened was unforgiveable… that was what she pounded into her head the most.

Yet there Mikaiya was, looking like a sad, lovesick puppy for everyone to see.

Chapter 15

MIKAIYA

If Mik had any doubts about Ariana getting her bouquet in a timely manner, she could eradicate them now. Yup. She had. Right in front of God and Paradise Valley.

This was an actual nightmare, wasn't it?

She had not counted on an audience. Nor had she counted on Ariana having the day off. The plan was for the flowers to be delivered to her house for her to find when she arrived home. Whenever that was. By then, Mik was supposed to be back in *her* house, where she could batten down the hatches and turn off her phone out of fear that she had once and for all ruined anything between them. Nope! Instead, she looked down the barrel of a metaphorical gun that was about to blow off her face. She simply didn't know who was holding the gun.

The audience, who tittered among themselves to see such beautiful drama erupting before them?

Skylar, who refused to let Mikaiya run the rest of the way home?

...Ariana?

I'm so sorry. This time, she wasn't apologizing for what happened ten years ago. She was telling both herself and her ex-girlfriend that *this wasn't supposed to happen.* Since when did Paradise Valley light the town fires so every bit of lesbian drama was aired out in public? Why the *hell* had the deliverywoman – there! there she was, getting a freaking coffee! – dropped the flowers off here? This wasn't supposed to happen! Mik was going to die!

The door opened. Bells jingled, and the wooden OPEN sign clacked against the glass. Heaven leaned in the doorway, arms crossed and a smirk the size of Wolf's Hill grazing her angular face. "You wouldn't happen to know who gave Ariana these pretty flowers, would you, Mik?" she asked.

Big words from a woman who once played softball with Mikaiya!

Saturday afternoon was the worst. Families off work and school. Tourists in town from the bigger cities. Sometimes the weather got its act together and brought a sunny paradise to the valley. There wasn't a drop of rain now. Instead, the sun gracefully took its place in the sky, illuminating the exact spot where Mikaiya and Skylar stood in front of Heaven's Café. Mik saw her own reflection before she made out Ari's bulky figure on the other side of the window. Hell, she saw the likes of Anem Singer before she recognized Ari's jacket. All the sun did was make this worse. Everyone was in too good of a mood to get the hell home, and people approaching them from either side stopped to see what the commotion was about on Main Street.

The number of people who recognized Mik and Ari was the #1 reason Mikaiya dreaded coming back to the small town that raised her. *All right, the #2 reason.*

Number one was glaring at her.

"Go on!" Skylar hissed. "Your chance!"

Mik didn't know what that meant. Time had slowed to a still. Was her heart still beating? Or was she better off jabbing her fist into her eye? It would feel about as good as staring at the woman she still couldn't get over.

Didn't help that Paradise Valley closed in all around them, that place they called home, for better or worse. *The only way this could be worse is if we were trapped on the grounds of Clark High.* Yet Main Street was where it all ended. They weren't too far from the place Mik was supposed to meet her girlfriend so they could run away and declare their eternal love to one another.

That same love now bubbled in her heart, but it was so acidic that it coated her throat in an ill-ease that made her want to vomit.

Well, if she was going to puke, she might as well have a good reason for making such a mess in the middle of the street.

"Excuse me." That was the only thing she said between pushing herself into the crowded café and standing before Ariana, who was more trapped than a fly in some spider's web. She looked like she was ready to die at any moment. The bouquet's handwritten note was clenched in her hand.

A few people parted to give Mik admittance to the table. She locked eyes with Ari and was reminded why she had once loved her so much.

There was life in her eyes. Breath. Soul. Fire. Mikaiya could pull any word she admired out of her ass and pretend it was gold. Didn't stop the memories of that first day they had a full conversation in high school. *I closed my locker door and saw those eyes. They glowed so brightly for a girl who was otherwise plain and lanky.* It turned out that they glowed with puppy love for the school's rising softball star. Ariana was the one who approached the other first. She once explained it as, "*I couldn't have lived with myself if I didn't try. I never expected you to ask me out later that week... it was like a dream come true.*"

That same luminosity greeted her now. The fire may have dulled to mere embers, but Mik still saw it. The love that Ari harbored in her hardened heart.

"Can we talk?" Mikaiya finally managed to spit, although her throat was so dry she considered it a miracle.

Ariana glanced at the faces surrounding them – and at the bouquet separating their familiar faces. "Do I have a choice?"

"You could say no. I'll leave."

Heaven slammed the café door shut and barred it with her body.

"Good luck with that," Ari said with a sniffle. Oh, no. The flowers! She was allergic, wasn't she? That's why her eyes were red, too. How could Mikaiya forget that her ex was allergic to lilies? *Are those white flowers actually lilies? Or just called that? I have no idea!* Mik second-guessed everything she said and did right now. Things had never been so dire since coming back to Paradise Valley. Her grandmother's illness didn't compare to this. Abby would recover, as her stubborn soul always did. Yet who could say if this relationship ever had another chance in hell?

"I'm sorry, Ari."

"You've said that a lot this month."

Mik swallowed the other apologies she had prepared in the past few seconds. *This isn't how everything was supposed to happen.* She met the eyes of every spectator, half of whom were amused and curious gals, while the other half cracked their knuckles in warning. More than one of them looked pretty damn keen to teach Mikaiya Marcott a *real* lesson if Ariana wasn't up to it.

"Yeah, I've said a lot of things. All of it's been the truth."

Ariana plucked a yellow petal off one of the roses. "The hell is this, anyway? Did living in the city make your so-called romantic creativity soft?"

"Blame her." Mik gestured to her best friend, still standing outside. Skylar looked away the moment she realized she was being called out. Nobody actually believed she was enamored with the weekly newspaper, yes? "She told me I needed to come up with some grand gesture, whatever that means."

Someone snorted behind Mik. It was probably Anem. She seemed the type to know what "grand gesture" meant.

"Your kind of grand gesture terrifies me, frankly. You think I don't remember the last one?"

"*Ooh, burn.*"

Mikaiya mentally blocked the comments from the audience. "I know all about yours, too. Like making out with me at the top of Wolf's Hill?" She paused for effect. "This past Tuesday?"

Ariana could have denied it, but her paling, sickly face announced to everyone else that Mik spoke the truth. *Ha! Suck it!* Ari wasn't getting out of this one without everyone knowing that this push-and-pull they played went both ways. Even if Ari's intention was to toy with and break Mikaiya's heart, she still felt something deep enough inside of her to go through that much. Mik would take it as a win. A win for posterity... and a win for her heart.

"Why you gotta bring that up?" Ariana positioned the bouquet so Mik struggled to see her ex-girlfriend's face. "That was a moment of weakness."

"Weakness my ass! You still like me!"

"I don't like anyone! Ask all of these assholes! I don't date!"

"That's a lie," Heaven said. "What she means is that she doesn't date for *long*. You should see all the girls she hangs out with in here..."

"Shut up, Heaven."

"You've got some big mouth on you, hon!" Heaven tugged on her apron, her frizzy hair brushing against the doorframe as she spun around and interjected herself into the conversation. "I remember when you barely came up to my tits. You wanna go?"

"No, I don't." Ari attempted to get out of her seat, but was so surrounded that even if Anem and the others wanted to let her go, they couldn't. Especially if Heaven refused to move. "And, obviously, things have changed. I no longer come up to only your tits. Nor am I the scrawny weakling everyone used to push around." That was directed at Mik. "Excuse me. I want to go home."

At first, Mikaiya did not move. Not until she had the chance to say, "I'm sorry, Ari," one last time.

Ariana scrunched her brows into a castrating scowl. "Sorry ain't enough, Mikkie. I don't care about the truth. Don't care that you're back in town. Just leave me alone."

That look on Ari's visage was the only reason Mik finally moved out of the way, head low and so embarrassed that she was definitely never, *ever* leaving the house again. She was also having a serious talk with Skylar about what it meant to meddle in someone else's love life. She'd be damned if it ever happened again.

"Thanks." That was the last thing she heard Ari say before the café door opened and closed. The silence she left behind made Mik want to scream.

"Whoa," one of the women behind her uttered. "Savage."

"All right, ladies. Show's over." Heaven waved everyone away from the table at the front of the café, let alone the door leading outside. Murmurs filled the air as Mik was left alone with the bouquet and Ari's abandoned to-go cup.

Skylar came into the café, disappointment on her face.

"Sorry, Mik," she mumbled.

"Yeah, well..." Mikaiya let out a mighty sigh. "It wasn't meant to be, I guess..."

Skylar picked up the crumpled note left behind. "Was she crying?"

"What are you talking about?"

Mik was handed the note. "It's kinda wet. See there? Looks like a tear."

"No way. Ari's not the kind of girl who cries all over some note from ghosts of girlfriends past."

"Did she used to be?"

That made Mikaiya double-take. "What would you know about how she used to be?"

"I only know that she's changed a lot. How?"

How, indeed?

Mikaiya plucked the to-go cup off the table and showed herself out of the café. She didn't wait for Skylar to catch up, or for Heaven to ask her what the hell she thought she was doing. *Killing myself. That's what it feels like.* It probably *was* suicide to follow Ariana to her house two blocks away. Unfortunately for Ari, Mikaiya knew where she lived, thanks to that truck conspicuously parked on Florida Street.

Whatever Ari had ordered in the café was probably cold by the time Mik reached the house, but it gave her an excuse to knock on the door and steel herself.

"What the hell do you *want?*"

That bellow nearly knocked Mik over when Ariana flung open the door. The only change between the café and now? Ariana had tossed aside her jacket. For the first time since returning to Paradise Valley, Mik got a grand view of *how* her ex had transformed herself from skinny thing to muscular EMT. *Holy shit. Those are muscles. Like, defined muscles.* Mik was damn speechless for a good five seconds. Long enough for her to remember she had a drink in her hand.

"You left this back at the café."

Ari yanked it out of Mik's hand. "I should throw this in your face."

Mik squeezed her eyes shut. "Then go ahead and do it." She waited a few moments, until she realized Ariana wasn't actually going to coat her ex's face in coffee and foam.

"If I threw hot coffee into your face," Ari growled, "who do you think would get called to take you to the hospital?"

"Your… coworkers?" Was that a trick question? Ariana obviously had the day off.

Rolling her eyes, Ari threw open the door and tugged on Mik's arm. "Get the hell in here. Sit down." She all but tossed her ex onto the couch by the front – yet curtained – window. "No. Stop talking. I don't want to hear more of your silly apologies. I want you to listen to what *I* have to say, for once."

Mik sucked in her bottom lip. Her ass was still recovering from the impact of hitting the couch like a space shuttle crashing into the ocean.

"I have spent the past ten years *dealing* with the aftermath of you skipping town, Mik. It's not only about us. It ain't only about people pitying me or wondering what I must have done to make you run away. You don't get it. When you left town, *everyone* felt it. Maybe I was the one most affected. Who gives a shit? Fact of the matter is, I don't think you properly understand what..."

"I understand."

Ariana stopped talking, her countenance conveying the ire of a woman never allowed to say her peace. "You do, huh? What exactly do you understand?"

Mik cleared her throat. "I understand that running away didn't solve a damn thing. I hurt us both when I did that. Obviously, I broke your heart, and I will spend the rest of my life apologizing for leaving you behind like..."

"Less about me, more about you."

"Right." Another heavy breath escaped Mik's lips. "These past ten years haven't been emotionally easy for me. The way I threw myself into my 'new' life was unhealthy. How it affected my love life was unhealthier. I heard what Heaven said about your own dating life. I don't... I don't think we've ever gotten over each other."

Ariana scoffed.

"I'm serious. That's why it's now or never, Ari." Mik stood up. *We're still the same height, at least*. Mik may have been the more muscular one back in the day, but Ari hadn't grown much since high school. Not in stature, anyway. "We can't simply ignore each other to death for the rest of our lives. We have to decide, right now, whether we're totally broken up or still harboring some weird, old puppy love for each other."

Ariana took a step back. "Thought you said the other day that it was 'real.'"

Really? She was doing this? Further proof that Ari might still have feelings for her ex-girlfriend. Why else would she play these games with Mik? *Maybe I deserve a few head-scratching games, but they have to end at some point*. She was inclined to finish them today.

"It *was* real, Ari." A moment of heavy silence settled between them. Breath fumed through

Mik's nostrils. Her palms sweat, and before she could wipe them against her jeans, she was reminded that the last time her hands sweated this badly was when she first told Ariana that she loved her. "I loved you, okay? I broke my own heart when I ran away like a cowardly git." She bowed her head. How could she look Ari in the eyes when so much shame settled over her? "I've spent the last two ten years thinking about what happened."

The sigh swimming between them wasn't one of tired exasperation. That was Ariana conceding defeat. To herself? To Mikaiya? To the universe that conspired to ruin such a good thing? Mik didn't know.

"You ain't no coward," Ari finally said. "I visited your grandma earlier today. She made me realize how scared you must have been for us. I'll always wish you said something, but... a coward? It probably took a lot of nerve to pack up your shit so quickly and get the hell out of town if you thought it meant saving our lives."

Life drained from Mik's face. "You saw my grandma today?"

"Yeah. Went to see how she's doing. She's pretty damn lucid for someone who had another stroke the other day."

Mik couldn't help but chuckle. "I can only aspire to be as spry as her when I'm her age. Never mind lucid. I think she hogged all the good genes in my family, because I sure as hell didn't get many." As for her mother and uncle... well, they died young, hadn't they?

Whatever good nature she had summoned in that cozy living room died when Ariana clasped her hands against her arms and looked away, a dour countenance claiming the air around her. "I'm sorry, too. Guess I spent so much time forcing myself to move on that when you came back to town without any warning... it set me for a spin, you know? Suddenly I had to think about everything I felt way back then. People were lookin' at me weird again. Not to mention, you come back here looking like a pretty city girl..."

"Don't remind me. You'd think nobody in Paradise Valley has ever seen brand-new Doc Marten's." Meanwhile, they hardly made her special in Portland. Half her office wore them. The other half wore Converse. There was the one random guy who wore Nike's, but only because his wife was an engineer at the head campus. Then again, shoe brands didn't mean much to people in Paradise Valley. All they cared about was how comfy and sturdy they were for all the brush clearing and hiking they did.

"I'm serious, Mik," Ariana continued, a touch of blush on her cheeks. "You look really good. Guess it kinda pissed me off. Why couldn't you come back to town looking like a serious mess? Could've given me a nice ego boost to know I looked better than you now."

Mik almost guffawed. "What are you talking about? You've always looked better than me!" Before Ariana could debate that, she continued, "You used to wear all those cute dresses and was always doing stuff to your hair! Now you got like... *muscles* and look like you could carry me from here to the library without breaking a sweat!"

"There's a way I could do that, yeah."

"Lift with your knees?"

Ariana slowly shook her head in amusement. "Good to see you're as silly as ever."

I mean, I wouldn't mind seeing her try to pack me off somewhere. Mik kept that thought to herself. "So, what are we going to do?"

"You mean besides hash this out every time we bump into one another?"

"I'd rather not, if it's all right with you. I would like to be able to show my face around town. It's bad enough my friend Skylar has heard ten different versions of 'our' story since she came here weeks ago. Did you know I dumped you for a dude?"

Ari shrugged. "For all I knew, you had."

That hit Mikaiya right in her heart. *I really left her with nothing*. Mik had spent so much of the past ten years convincing herself that she had done the right thing, that Ariana had surely moved on sooner rather than later, that her uncle's threats wouldn't haunt them for the rest of their lives...

Was it any wonder they were still torn up over one another?

Ariana took a step toward Mik. *Well, here it comes. Time for us to end this, I guess.* Mikaiya would at least do themselves the honor of keeping her head up and her pride somewhat intact. That was the adult thing to do. Mature. Yeah. *Mature.*

"I still love you."

Nope. Mikaiya had not been expecting to hear that. "What?"

Ari broke eye contact. Her cheeks were so pink that Mikaiya was convinced her ex sucked the vitality right out of her. It also explained the swaying back and forth that commenced when Ariana debated a plethora of thoughts in her head.

"Don't make me say it again," Ari all but whispered. "Know how embarrasin' that is?"

Mik could hardly believe her ears. "You… love me? Still?"

"You ain't exactly an easy gal to get over."

That deadpan tone somehow made Mik giddier than ever. "I mean, I don't wanna toot my own horn or anything, but I figure that *really* has to make me pretty special, so…"

For the second time that week, Ariana pulled Mik into her arms and reminded her that someone knew how to kiss as well as ever.

Chapter 16

MIKAIYA

The woman sure knew how to run her mouth, huh? *Some things never, ever change!* Ariana must take that to heart if she didn't want to get hurt again. Just because some people matured and changed for the better didn't mean *everything* got better. Mikaiya Marcott was probably destined to be that woman who gabbed everyone's ear off once they got her attention. She would also have that magic ability to pry her mouth open and insert her foot like she was the most talented contortionist in Paradise Valley – and there were quite a few of those!

Good thing Ari knew the best way to shut that mouth up for a few minutes.

It was like the old days. Only instead of Ariana succumbing to nervous giggles the first few times she kissed her biggest crush at school, she now commanded the space around them. Mikaiya was the one turning into the puddle of mush as she hastily flung her arms around Ari's broad shoulders and dove head first into a kiss big enough to knock them both off their feet.

This was different from the rainy day atop Wolf's Hill. Ariana had an agenda then. She wanted to remember what it was like to kiss Mikaiya Marcott... and see that look of pain on her face when she realized it wasn't meant to be. There was no agenda now, outside of further proving how much a certain someone had changed.

Mikaiya wanted to make cute jokes about Ari carrying her across the room? They wouldn't be so funny if they actually came true!

"Whoa!" Mikaiya gave herself the hiccups from how deeply she swallowed that sound. Ari would have been pleased with herself if she weren't so busy "lifting from her knees" to ensure she didn't hurt herself when she heaved Mikaiya over her shoulder. Fists flew through the air. Feet kicked several feet away from Ari's face. A tight little butt was in her grasp. After ten years of misery, Ari couldn't think of a better way to show her appreciation than by smacking Mik's ass on their way down the hall.

"Keep putting up such a fuss and I'll spank you some more, Mik!"

"I ain't fussin'!"

That happy voice echoed in the narrow hallway. Ari kicked open her bedroom door. She had a feeling Mikaiya wouldn't be so affected by city living that she scoffed at a messy, unmade bed and a few dirty clothes on the floor. Wasn't like Ari was opening the blinds or turning on the lights, anyway. She planned on keeping Mik distracted from what one grown woman's bedroom looked like!

"Oh, wow, I like how this looks!" Ariana was the master of her miniature universe as she pulled Mik this way and pushed her *that* way on the double bed. She wasn't the first woman to find herself in Ariana's bed covers, but she was definitely the most satisfying to witness scrambling around, attempting to locate her lost bearings while assessing the situation. *I'm giving you what you deserve, Mik.* If Mikaiya were so serious about still having feelings for her ex, well... Ariana wasn't convinced Mikaiya would say no. To any of this.

It was, however, a sweet reversal from how sex used to look like between them.

"You're like a fish floppin' out of water, girl." Ari pulled her covers all the way back and lost her shirt over the top of her head. Yeah, she figured showing off her sports bra would calm Mik down long enough to give her the kind of heavy kiss that made a woman moan. "Do I gotta put a hook in your mouth?"

Mikaiya finally got a damn word out of her lips. "The hell are you talking about? That some code for tonguin' me?"

Not a half bad idea.

Mikaiya figured out her place in bed as soon as Ari's lips were back on hers. The urgency they had suppressed all week finally came to a serious head. There was no turning back. Ariana's only hope was to make this the sweetest yet hottest lovemaking she ever entertained, whether in her own bed or someone else's.

A flood of memories came back to her as she continued to kiss, touch, and woo the ghost that had come back to town as if nothing had ever happened. Memories that unlocked the warmest parts of Ariana's life… and the coldest. Hot nights in the locker room showers, in each other's rooms, and in the loft of her uncle's barn. Cold nights huddled together in the rain as they waited for their ride to pick them up from softball practice, hiking up Wolf's Hill in the dead of winter, or drowning in ice cubes on warm summer nights. Team parties full of cheap booze, pot, and a dozen young gay girls swapping spit and stories. Playing Seven Minutes in Heaven and ensuring they got each other by carefully calculating the rotation of the empty beer bottle. Dressing up for prom like they were going to their own wedding. Arguing with Abby whether they really knew what they were doing or not. Chasing chickens in a neighbor's yard for a whole five bucks. Returning library books so late that the computer system couldn't figure out how much to charge them. Looking up naughty videos on the internet and wondering how those pretty ladies could finger each other with such sharp nails. Trying on each other's clothes and laughing because they looked so ridiculous.

Sharing a kiss for the first time.

Touching one another for the first time.

Kissing one last time after the graduation ceremony was over.

There was a picture of that moment, taken on a disposable Kodak camera, shoved somewhere in the depths of Ariana's desk. She hadn't looked at it in years, but she remembered what it looked like. Her arm around Mik, eyes squeezed shut as she happily tilted her chin toward the ceiling. Black hair in a thin ponytail creating a blur effect with the bright gym lights shining above. Mikaiya's happy smile pressing a half-finished kiss into her girlfriend's cheek.

It had been the last time Ariana was truly happy, let alone as her old self.

I love you. I really do. Maybe that was her downfall, her Achilles heel, the stupid thing that would end her life as early as Uncle Jake's. At least she wouldn't go down full of hate and vitriol. She'd rather die a fool in love.

Gleaning a single ounce of what she used to feel would make this worth it.

She made love to her ex-girlfriend as if she were proving to the universe that not only was she okay, she was *thriving*. A kiss to the throat was met with such a gasp that Ariana could no longer hold back from touching places she hadn't felt in a decade. Mikaiya may have aged into a full-grown adult, but she was still much the same in so many delightful ways. It wasn't only familiarity she offered, however. It was new, raw experiences that they couldn't have known when they were kids.

The room was darker from the setting sun by the time Ari finally fell to one side. Mikaiya didn't hesitate to fling herself on top of her lover, the kisses as strong and the touches as merciless as they had been on the other end. Ari's only regret was that they were too busy kissing all the time to make enough noise to scandalize the neighbors, let alone any roommates coming home a little too early.

Ariana didn't care. How could she give a single shit when that rush of adrenaline was coming back to her, one thrust at a time?

There were occasions when a woman was so drawn into the moment that she never fully came back to her senses until the fun was long over. That's what happened to Ari as soon as she became so drunk on Mikaiya that one second seamlessly flowed into the next.

Wasn't I throwing you down onto my bed a moment before? That's what she thought as she sat up in her bed, naked, with another naked woman panting next to her. "Jeez," she said, both to her own brain and to Mik, who acted as if she had finished running a marathon. "Think you might need to start working out?"

"I ain't out of breath!" Mikaiya asserted. "I'm... sweaty... you pack a punch in your everything, okay?"

Ariana bent her knee and slung her arm over it. "Liked that, did you?" The memories were slowly returning. *Not bad, Ari. Not bad.* She had definitely learned a few things over the past ten years. So had Mik. Did that mean they had more to discover after their, ah… *break?*

Mikaiya flung herself back against the mattress. "I'd think all that screaming I did would tell you I liked it."

"I don't remember any screaming."

"Huh. Must've only been in my head."

Ari eased herself back down. Mik's body heat wasn't so far away, yet she couldn't bring herself to snuggle up next to it. Not yet. She needed a few more minutes to decompress and come to terms with her feelings.

It was one thing to have sex. Quite another to *cuddle.*

"So what happens now?" Mik asked.

Ari continued to stare at her ceiling for a few more seconds, debating what words to use, the tone, how to say, "*Whatever you want to happen,*" without sounding too desperate or too indifferent.

She ended up saying, "We start over again."

There were a million meanings to such a simple phrase. Ariana wasn't in the mood to parse them quite yet. Neither was Mik, who slowly turned onto her side and buried her face into the crook of her lover's arm. They went from politely avoiding too much sentimentality to fully embracing it in the span of a few minutes.

Starting over again might be the death of them at that rate. Then again, it finely mirrored how it all began back in high school, when a single kiss led to a little more – then much more.

Here was to hoping that they were still the same crazy kids in all the right ways. And had changed for the better in all the right ways, too. Hope was the biggest thread spinning them together now. The fact Ariana held so much hope in her heart almost made it worth it.

Chapter 17

MIKAIYA

The café door slammed shut, jostling the bells and accidentally turning the Open/Close sign around. The man sauntering in to order an after-hours decaf didn't notice what he had done until his wife patted him on the shoulder and scolded him for being so inconsiderate.

Come on, Ari, where are you? Mik's coffee continued to chill in her hands. It didn't matter how high Heaven cranked the heater in her café. A recent cold snap had sheeted Paradise Valley in ice, and while many of the locals were accustomed to navigating these colder months among the Coast Range, it didn't mean they looked forward to going out in their bundled jackets, scarves, and hats. Mik shivered in her thick gray sweater and scarf tucked deep into the collar. Or maybe those chills came from a different place. A place of insecurity.

She was supposed to meet Ariana that night, as soon as the EMT finished her shift. Whenever that would be. At five to five, Ari had texted Mikaiya to tell her she was still at the county hospital and would probably be late to their date. If they could call this a date.

No. It's a date. She called it one when she texted me about getting coffee last night. Mik steadied her breathing as she pretended to be enamored with scrolling her Reddit feed. She liked keeping up with the goings-on back in Portland. Which was why she was *totally* reading posts and not simply scrolling endlessly in a futile attempt to stay preoccupied.

The people surrounding her, staring at her over their cups of coffee and laptops, absolutely did not help. One of the more curious patrons was the woman with a headscarf, who was often seen in Heaven's Café clacking away at her

MacBook. Piles of well-worn notebooks, library books, and print-outs surrounded her little workstation. Mikaiya struggled to see a small cup of tea in the midst of that organized chaos. By then, however, she had caught the woman's attentions, and all Mik could think about was how this same person was there when Ariana received her bouquet of flowers.

Those roses were still going strong on the front counter, where Heaven had put them to good use as a festive decoration for her café. The few times Mik had shown her face again were marked with sarcastic, *"Thanks for the donation! Everyone loves the roses, Mik!"* followed with chuckles that almost ran Mikaiya out of the café. Yet she knew that was Heaven's way of chiding her for being the Town Dumbass. Besides, it wouldn't be a gallant return to her home turf if her old softball teammates from high school didn't give her shit. Heaven was the upperclassman who helped "initiate" Mik and Ari's class by leading them all into a hayfield for a "special practice" that turned into being stranded for five hours.

Not bitter, Heaven. Some things never changed from college. Heaven may have bought and renovated this place while Mikaiya was gone, becoming one of the youngest brick-and-mortar shop owners in Paradise Valley, but she was still ruthless. *Huh. Must be how she came into the money.*

Mik politely looked away from the woman working on her laptop and caught the moment Ariana finally walked into the place.

"Uh oh," Heaven muttered, her gaze snapping between Ari and Mik as if things were about to blow up again. Or, more likely, she was about to gain another bouquet in her café.

Yet Ari briefly said hello to someone sitting at the front window before making her way to Mik's table. She ripped off her jacket and, without a formal greeting, plopped it on the back of the empty chair and offered her date a wink. *I'd be winking, too!* She was still wearing her EMT shirt beneath, and those were muscles flexing in the dim light of the cozy café.

Score one for me having sex with that? Mikaiya had never felt more like the cute tomboy who was absolutely precious in her flannel and short haircut when she was next to the new and upgraded Ariana. That may have been another reason her relationships in Portland never went anywhere. Not only was she meant to be romancing the locals in her hometown, but she was meant to be with a woman who wasn't afraid to throw her weight!

Heaven checked her gaping mouth when Ari turned around to order her drink. To Mik's mild surprised, her girlfriend asked for something with caffeine in it. Was she planning to stay up all night? Didn't she have another shift in twelve hours? *Oh, my God. She's dragging me back to her place later, isn't she?* Wouldn't be the first time they fooled around with the roommates down the hall and Ariana's alarm threatening to go off. They had kept the hookups to a minimum that past week and a half while they "started over."

Maybe the minimum was no longer enough?

"What?" Ari asked, when she sat down and caught the look on Mik's face. "Do I got something on my face?"

The corner of Mik's mouth twitched. She had to seriously refrain from quipping, "*I dunno, my pussy?*" They were in public, after all. Polite freakin' company!

"No, just... you look great?"

"Oh. So it's flattery." She said that with a sigh, yet she leaned back, one leg angled over the other and a smug satisfaction taking her over. Ever since they rekindled their romance – and that included on the summit of Wolf's Hill, Mik supposed – Ari had taken control of most of the flirtations, and used her confidence to her greatest advantage. There were the signs of the sweet girl Mik used to know, and she got a *great* view of it when their usual conversations devolved into pillow talk... but sometimes Mikaiya swore she was dating a brand-new person.

Rather exciting, wasn't it? Maybe a role reversal was exactly what they needed now that they were almost thirty.

"I'm told I'm great at flattery." Mikaiya looked around the room again. "Is it me, or is everyone staring at us?"

"Play it cool. Act like we've been married for ten years. The novelty will wear off pretty soon."

Heaven called out Ari's drink, and Mik was temporarily left to her own devices on the bench lining the café's far wall. She caught a look from the woman at her MacBook again. Eventually, she would learn the stranger's name, but for now, she was merely some woman staring at Mik as if she were a *god.*

Okay, maybe not a god, but definitely someone who knew what she was about, huh?

"So…" Ari sat back down with her hazelnut latte, something Mikaiya had quickly come to learn was her girlfriend's favorite caffeinated treat. "Let's start with how college worked out for you. Don't hold anything back. I want to hear about every crying fit over grades and every drunken night you now regret."

Mikaiya may have been caught off guard by how suddenly the tone shifted, but she had been prepared for the invasive questions. Part of getting back together was acknowledging that the past was in the past – but that didn't mean they didn't want to know everything about each other's twenties, since they were curious to catch up now that the negative emotions had dimmed. Besides, didn't couples talk about their pasts and what made them the people they were today? Their last date, which also happened to be their first *official* date since getting back together, was all about Ariana airing out her community college experience and what it was like becoming an EMT. Mikaiya had been so fascinated that she totally forgot to talk about her first major job interview and how she threw up both before and after.

They stayed until the café closed at eight, but they were far from the last couple in the place. Turned out that Heaven's had become one of the biggest hangout spots for the local gay women who liked to have public meetups, dates, and other such get-togethers. It helped that Heaven understood them well, although Mik had always assumed her old teammate was straight. Wasn't there something about an ex-husband? Not that it meant anything in Paradise Valley.

“Do you want to go back to Portland?”

Mikaiya was caught by surprise. Her attentions were elsewhere, such as the way Heaven started closing up shop and one girl in the corner looked an awful lot like Reese Witherspoon, but with red hair. *First actress crush. Ugh. Remember when we used to watch “Legally Blonde” every weekend, Ari?*

“I dunno,” Mik finally said. “It had its ups and downs, but I mostly stayed there because I had a job, and I didn’t know where else to go.” She shrugged. “Obviously I had made friends there, but it’s the kind of place that can really get you down if you’re not suited for it. Lots of problems right in your face, you know?”

Ari nodded. “So I’ve heard.”

“You’d go nuts as an EMT in Portland. Probably.” Ariana often complained about the downtime in their county, but she would burn out so quickly in the city. She was better off waiting for the occasional fall or stroke, two things the Marcotts were great at summoning. Abby was finally home from the hospital and recuperating at record pace, but Mik wouldn’t deny that she loved having an EMT for a girlfriend. Who knew when that would come in handy in their personal life? "I don't pretend to speak for what a badass you are these days."

"I kind of am a badass," Ari said with a sniff. "I carried your ass to the hospital, didn't I?"

Mik blushed. "That's not the only place you like carrying me."

"Hmm?" Ari checked the time on her phone. "They're going to close up soon. You wanna head back to my place, or does your grandmother need you at yours?"

"She's doing fine with just Skylar and the nurse there, if that's what you're asking."

"So then you *really* wanna come back?"

"Depends. You carrying me back to your bedroom again?"

"Dunno. I had to lift a 300 pound man onto a stretcher three hours ago. Might need a serious soak in the tub first. Or a nice massage. You know anyone handing those out?"

Mikaiya could hardly contain her rolling eyes. "Put some food in my stomach, and we'll see where it goes."

Ari headed to the bathroom while Mikaiya texted Skylar to let her know she probably wouldn't be home that night. "*That's right, slut, get it!*" Not how Mik would have put it, but she appreciated the sentiment. She was very much in the business of "getting it," but had a feeling Ariana would be in control of how that manifested tonight.

Worked for Mik!

"Ready?" Ari threw on her jacket and motioned toward the door, now rightfully saying CLOSED to the outside world. She was halfway to taking Mikaiya's hand on their way out when she stopped, backtracked to the café counter, and grabbed the vase of flowers.

"Hey!" Heaven chided. "Those are my donations!"

"I believe they actually belong to me." Ari offered her a wave as Mik stepped out into the frigid night. "I'll take good care of them!"

"You better! They've been getting me some nice tips!"

Ari carefully positioned the vase of roses into the center seat of her truck. Mikaiya slowly shook her head as she buckled up and waited for the heater to blast into life. She needed it. Her poor knuckles were numb! "Thought you were allergic to lilies?"

The truck roared to life. "Should be fine if I stick them on the dining table."

"Should be fine, she says..."

"You wanna get outta here or not? I hear there's pizza back at the house, and I'm cold."

"Me too. I swear it wasn't this cold when I got here a month ago."

Ari let the truck idle as she stared into the rearview mirror, chuckling. "You've never read King, right?"

"No. Although you're making compelling arguments for me to join a certain book club."

"There's this poem in *It*. You know, the one about the clown?"

Mikaiya nodded.

"There's this kid who likes this girl, so he writes a poem about her hair being like January embers. Really nice."

"What's that got to do with us going back to eat pizza and take a bath?"

"You ain't cold if you've got a little fire still burning inside of you."

The truck pulled out of its parking spot. *I have no idea what the hell that means*. Mik merely shook her head, Ariana driving as if she were the luckiest – and the warmest – woman in the world. Or, at least, in Paradise Valley.

Eventually, Mikaiya smiled. Maybe she got it, after all.

Hildred Billings is a Japanese and Religious Studies graduate who has spent her entire life knowing she would write for a living someday. She has lived in Japan a total of three times in three different locations, from the heights of the Japanese alps to the hectic Tokyo suburbs, with a life in Shikoku somewhere in there too. When she's not writing, however, she spends most of her time talking about Asian pop music, cats, and bad 80's fantasy movies with anyone who will listen…or not.

Her writing centers around themes of redemption, sexuality, and death, sometimes all at once. Although she enjoys writing in the genre of fantasy the most, she strives to show as much reality as possible through her characters and situations, since she's a furious realist herself.

Currently, Hildred lives in Oregon with her girlfriend, with dreams of maybe having a cat around someday.

Connect with Hildred on any of the following:

Website: http://www.hildred-billings.com
Twitter: http://twitter.com/hildred
Facebook: http://facebook.com/authorhildredbillings
Tumblr: http://tumblr.com/hildred

Made in the USA
Monee, IL
24 March 2020

23582849R00136